NIKOLAI
THE SYNDICATES BOOK IV

Cala Riley

Copyright @ 2022 by Cala Riley All rights reserved. No part of this publication may be reproduced, distributed, or transmitted in any form or by any means without the prior written consent of the publisher, except brief quotes used for reviews and certain other non-commercial uses, as per copyright laws. This is a work of fiction. Names, characters, businesses, places, events and incidents are either the products of the author's imagination or used in a fictitious manner. Any resemblance to actual persons, living or dead, or actual events is purely coincidental.

Nikolai Cover Photo by: Books and Moods

Editing by: My Brothers Editor

Dedication:
To Elle. You are the best decision we ever made.
We appreciate all the love and care you put into each edit.
You are a rockstar woman!

PROLOGUE

Lia

"And they lived happily ever after."

I smile up at my mom as she closes the book before setting it on my nightstand.

"I want a prince just like the one in the story."

She chuckles as she leans down to tuck me into bed.

"What about the prince do you like so much?" she asks.

"He's brave and strong. He could protect me from all the monsters," I tell her seriously.

Ever since Frankie at school told me about the monsters that like to hide in closets and under beds, I've been scared to sleep alone. Mom bought me a nightlight and checks for them every night for me, but if I had a prince, he would get rid of them for good.

"Oh honey. I told you there are no monsters in your closet or under your bed. Frankie was trying to scare you and look, it worked. You can't respond the way people expect you to all the time. Especially if they are trying to get a rise out of you." She tucks a piece of hair behind my ear. "One day you'll get your prince, but he might not be a prince at all. He may be exactly what you always hoped for, or he might be unexpected. All I know is that he won't be this picture-perfect man in your head. They only exist in fairy tales."

"Will he protect me?" I ask in a small voice.

"If he doesn't, then he doesn't deserve your heart. Never accept less than you're worth, Lia. That means someone who will protect and care for you, but you will also do the same for them in return. As much as you take from them, you must also give. That's the key to a good relationship."

"Is that what you had with Daddy?"

Her eyes grow sad. "It was."

"I miss him."

"Me too. Every single day."

"I'll find me a good prince and treat him as great as he treats me."

"Good. Then your dear old mom won't have to worry about you. Now, get to sleep."

She leans down, kissing my forehead. I smile up at her.

"I love you, Mama."

"I love you too, Lia."

CHAPTER ONE

Lia

I hear a noise outside my door. The same noise I have heard every night since I came here.

Feet shuffling. The twist of a knob. A soft curse. Then ambling away.

Only tonight they don't leave. Instead, I hear a key turning in the lock.

My heart beats erratically, and I freeze. I don't know what to do.

I hear the door open and his footsteps coming closer. The bed dips as he sits on the edge.

I close my eyes tighter. Maybe if I just pretend to sleep, he will go away. He won't do what he's thinking about doing.

As soon as his hand touches my shoulder, I flinch. So much for pretending to sleep.

"My sweet Felicity. I know you are awake. Why have you been hiding from me?"

I cringe at the sound of his voice. He has finally lost it. I jump out the opposite side of the bed and back toward the window. I can barely see him in the darkness. I squeeze my fingers tight around the knife I have in my hand. I keep it under my pillow just in case of something just like this. I could pretend nothing was going to happen when he would just hover outside the door. But now he has finally gone too far. I need to get out of here now.

"Come on, Felicity. Stop playing games. Come here, dear." He tries to soften his voice to coax me back toward him as he stands from the bed. My only problem is that he is between me and the door. I try to pull up on the window behind me, but it is locked. I can't unlock it without drawing his attention.

"Charles. I need to sleep. You should go back to your bed and Sheila. Won't she miss you?" I say softly, hoping to keep things calm as I inch my way to my closet. If I can keep him focused, I might make it to the door.

"She took her sleeping pill an hour ago. The house could burn down, and she'd sleep through it. Now we have time for us. I've seen the way you look at me when no one is watching. I know you want me too."

Think, Felicity.

"Charles. I think there has been a miscommunication. I'm only seventeen." I keep my voice soft. If he is right, Sheila wouldn't hear me scream. The neighbors in this neighborhood keep to themselves, so while they would peek out of their windows, they would act like they didn't see or hear anything.

"Only for a couple more days," he replies.

I inch along the wall my closet is on. If I can get close enough, he left the bedroom door open. I just need to be able to run through it and I might make it out of the front door.

He takes two steps toward me, and I stop. He stares at me, looking to see what my next move is. I decide it's make it or break it time. I need to at least try. I can tell by the look in his eye, he's not letting me out of this room voluntarily.

I push off the wall, rushing toward the door. I almost make it through when I feel him latch on to my hair and pull me back, flinging me onto the floor.

"Silly girl," he tsks. "I was going to be nice and gentle, but now I guess I will have to be rough." He grabs a hold of my hair again and pulls me up onto the bed. I struggle to get away, but he is stronger than me. He still hasn't noticed the knife in my hand. This is my last hope.

I go slack underneath him.

"That's a good girl. Maybe I won't punish you too bad after all."

He runs his nose along my neck, making me shudder in disgust.

"Mm. You smell wonderful. Do you know how bad you have teased me these last couple of months?" He pushes his crotch into me and I feel his bulge. I can feel the acid burning the back of my throat, wanting to come up, but I choke it back down. "You are going to be a sweet one, aren't you?"

I try one last attempt to get him to leave on his own. "You don't want to do this. I will tell them. I will tell everyone," I whisper to him.

"No, you won't. They wouldn't believe a foster teen with a record like yours. Even if they did, you would go missing before charges could be filed. They would classify you as just another runaway." He laughs at me.

I tried. I really did. I send a quick prayer up.

Please. Let me get out of this. Keep me safe.

My prayers have never been answered before, but it's worth trying.

Charles goes to lean down to kiss me. This is the moment I press the button on the switchblade, just like *she* taught me. I swing my hand up and stab him in the stomach. I pull back and stab again as he gasps. He jumps up and stumbles back into the wall. I don't wait another second. I fall off the bed, stumbling toward the door, and this time I make it through. I run down the hall past the kitchen and swing around the archway to the front door. It takes me a second to unlock the door, but I make it just in time to hear him stumble into the hall. I don't hesitate. I fling the door open and run. I keep running down the block and through some alleyways.

I don't even think twice about where I'm going. My body moving on autopilot, knowing where I need to go. Where I've planned on going for weeks. I keep running until I hear sirens headed in the opposite direction. I slow down to a jog as I continue on to my destination. Once I'm out of the neighborhood, I slow down to a walk. I have another two miles to go until I make it to where I am going. I just hope I remember the directions she gave me.

Once I get closer, I can feel the adrenaline spike in my system. I'm two streets away. I look along the concrete wall for the sign. She said she marked it with two fake roses mixed in with the vines covering the wall. I walk along it for a quarter of a mile before I see them, just like she said they would be. Moving the shrubs, I find the step ladder set up against the wall. I step up and glance over to the other side. Now it is a waiting game. I don't have my phone, so I have no idea what time it is.

She said every hour two men walk the grounds. She said once they round the east end of the building; I have forty-five minutes to get in before they make it back around. The building is massive. Instead of a house, this looks like a mansion. How many rooms are in this place? She wasn't kidding when she said she could hide me for weeks without anyone finding me. I look for the cameras she warned me about. I spot all three of them, each one exactly where she said they would be. I was nervous about trusting her at first, but it looks like she was telling me the truth.

I hear the laughter before I see them. Two tall men walking around the west end of the building. I duck down quickly so they don't see me.

"I swear that is what he said." I can hear the Russian accent as he speaks.

"Bullshit," the other one says.

"It is. You can ask Nikolai. He said it."

"If he did, he would not still be alive. Especially not if Nikolai is the one he said it to."

I can hear their voices grow fainter as they move farther away. I poke my head up to see where they are. I see them round the side of the building. I wait two minutes to make sure they are really gone.

I pull myself up onto the wall and push the ladder back into the bushes. I look around and make sure it is clear before I jump down. Once on the ground, I pause and look around again. Still no movement. I move toward the building and find the ladder that leads up to the second-story balcony. I quickly climb up and swing myself over onto the balcony. I walk to the door and try the handle. Unlocked. Just like she promised. I open the door quickly and slip in while shutting it. The lights are all off. I can't tell if she is in here.

I am just about to call out to her when I hear a gun hammer being pulled back. I freeze as the light flicks on. Out of the corner of my eye, I see the gun pointed right at my head. I can tell there is a figure behind it, but I'm focused on the gun. My heart racing.

"Who are you?" I hear his deep voice command.

"I-I-I'm sorry," I stumble over my words.

"I said, who are you?" He moves to stand in front of me and points the gun right at my face. He is only inches from me.

"I…" I gulp big.

"Stupid girl. Think you are brave sneaking into this house? Into *my* room?" He sneers while lowering the gun to my chest as his eyes peruse my body. I feel myself shaking.

I think I'm in shock.

It could be from the events of tonight, or it could be from him. This man reeks of power. He's standing there in nothing but boxer briefs, but even practically naked, he commands respect from those around him. Nikolai Petrov. Everyone in this city knows who he is.

"Did you sneak in here for a quick fuck?"

I snap out of it and narrow my eyes at him.

"You will do." He smirks at me.

"Absolutely not. I didn't even know this was your room." I fold my arms across my chest.

At my sudden movement, he raises his gun back to my face.

"What are you here for then?"

I can't tell him. She will get in trouble. I have to protect her. She's the only one who has ever tried to help me without expecting something in return.

"So you will stay silent then?"

My shaking hasn't stopped and as my adrenaline dissipates, I can feel myself getting weaker.

"How about I just kill you then, huh?" I can hear his voice, but it sounds like it is in a tunnel. I feel myself swaying.

"Just do it then." I hear myself say as my eyes roll back into my head. My last thought before I black out.

At least he didn't get me.

NIK

"WHAT THE FUCK?" I jump forward and grab the girl before she falls to the floor. I reach over and set my gun on the desk next to me.

I pick her up and take her to my bed. Pulling the covers back with one hand, I lay her down and step back.

I can't say that the girl isn't gorgeous. About five foot two, long brown hair and gorgeous blue eyes. It's like she was sent from heaven. Then she opened her mouth and gave me fire. I would be lying if I said it didn't get me hard. No one, especially not women, would dare speak to me in such a manner. It means certain death, but this girl did, and I didn't immediately want to kill her.

I take a closer look at her. Her hair is all tangled. Her face looks peaceful as she lies there. If I hadn't seen her fall myself, I would have just thought she was sleeping. As I continue to take in her appearance, I see that she has blood on her white tank top. I noticed it before, but I was more worried about why she was here.

I grab my phone off my nightstand and make a call.

"Security breach." I hang up as I dial the next number.

"Get to my room now."

It only been minutes, but that's all it took for me to start fuming. How could they have missed this young girl sneaking past us?

"Dimitri. How did this happen?" I gesture toward the girl on my bed.

He laughs. "You tell me, boss. How did a beautiful woman make it in your bed?"

I glare at him. "Through my window, apparently."

He gives me a look of confusion, then looks back at her.

"Is that blood?" he asks, pointing at her top.

"It looks like it. I didn't get much out of her before she passed out. Find out who she is."

"On it." He takes his phone out and snaps a picture of her. As he opens my door, my sister pushes her way in.

"Ivanna, what are you doing in here? You should be in the safe room."

"Nik. Call off the guards. I know how she got in and I know who she is."

"You had better start talking," I command.

"Her name is Felicity. She's a friend of mine from school. I told her how to get in without being detected. She got the rooms wrong. She was supposed to come to mine."

Ivanna walks over to the girl on my bed and sits next to her.

"What did you do to her?" I can hear the concern in her voice. Whoever this is, Ivanna cares for her.

"Nothing. She passed out while I was trying to figure out how she got in here. Why is she here? Someone surely misses her."

"Felicity's in foster care. She only had two days left and then she was going to leave her foster home and go to a homeless shelter. Her foster father kept making moves on her. She was scared to be at home." Ivanna looks over at me before looking back at her friend. "I gave her a switchblade and showed her how to use it. I told her that if he ever laid a finger on her, to use the blade, then come here. I promised her I would help protect her." Ivanna looks up with tears in her eyes. "If she is here, it means he tried something. I just hope he wasn't successful."

I feel myself getting angry.

Squeezing my phone, I dial another number. "Call off the lockdown. Debrief at sunrise. Be extra watchful," I bark into my phone. Turning to Dimitri, I demand, "Get the doctor here now. We need to check her out. Send Anton to the police and find out what they know. We need to get ahead of this."

As he leaves, I go to my closet and get dressed.

"Nik," I hear Ivanna call out. "What are you going to do to her?"

I finish getting dressed before I answer.

"Ivy," I sigh as I use her childhood nickname. "You took a risk bringing her here. If Dad were still alive, she'd already be dead, and you would be punished."

She stands, walking toward me, and hugs me. "Nik. She needs our help. This sick foster father is in his fifties. He has been touching her inappropriately. She tried to leave once, but he threatened to call the cops and report her as a runaway. She started avoiding home as much as she could instead."

"Why didn't she just call the cops herself or her caseworker? This is not our problem to be getting involved with, but you made it our problem." I run my hand through my hair. "Stupid girl," I whisper.

"I'm not stupid. She didn't call them because they didn't listen to her. She tried telling them in the beginning and they told her she was imagining things. That not every man who lays a hand on her is doing so sexually. They accused her of acting out. Why would she trust the system that let her down in the first place?" Ivanna says harshly.

I look at the girl. Felicity. I feel a draw to her. I walk to her and pick up her wrist as I check her pulse. I feel a steady heartbeat.

"We can discuss this later. Go to your room."

"No! I want to stay and make sure she is okay, and you don't do anything to her."

I turn to glare at her. I see her shrink away. "You will not disobey. Go to your room. I will do with her what I please."

Ivanna huffs, but she is smart enough to walk away. Few have the nerve to stand up to me, but that is the downfall of growing up with Ivanna. She's tough as nails and not always afraid of me.

I scroll through my phone as Dimitri and Dr. Daniil come in. Daniil gets right to work looking over Felicity.

"Dimitri filled me in. Her pulse is steady."

"We will stand right outside. I need a full body exam." I walk to my dresser and pull out a T-shirt and boxers. "Put these on her when she is done and leave the others on the floor."

He nods and we leave the room, shutting the door behind us.

"We need Ivanna to tell us if there are any other ways to get in or out. We need to rethink our security. This *can't* happen again," I say as I lean against the wall.

"Yes, boss. I will go talk to her now. Do you want me to set up a spare room for tonight?" I look at my watch and see it is close to four in the morning.

"No. The girl can sleep in my room while I work. Have you heard from

NIKOLAI

Anton yet?"

"Not yet. I will call and check in."

I dismiss him and glance back into the room.

What are you doing?

CHAPTER TWO

Lia

I go to move and almost fall off the bed. I moan as I start to move my legs.

Why am I so sore?

I open my eyes and panic. I sit straight up.

Where am I?

The events from the night before come flooding back. Charles. Nikolai. How am I not dead?

"You're awake. Good. I will have them prepare you food."

I follow the voice of the man sitting at the desk in the corner of the room. He hasn't even looked up from the computer he is working on.

I look down and notice my clothes have been changed. I gasp.

"What did you do to me while I was passed out?" I ask, trying to keep my voice steady.

"Nothing. I had our doctor change you when he did your exam."

"What exam? What the hell?"

The man leans back in his chair, giving me his undivided attention. "I had him look you over to be sure you weren't hurt. You are fine though."

"What does that even mean? Why am I not dead?" I frown.

His eyes cut to mine. "If you were smart, you would keep your mouth shut and not question your good luck."

I move farther back on the bed, crowding against the headboard as I curl my arms around my knees, pressing them to my chest. "I don't have good luck. I have the shittiest luck actually, so forgive me if I don't trust your intentions."

He stands from his desk, making his way toward the bed. My breath catches as he stands next to me, his large body looming over me.

"You made a mistake coming here. You don't get to ask questions. As of right now, all you need to know is you currently belong to me. Try not to make shit harder than it needs to be."

I swallow hard. "I know I made a mistake. If you show me the door, I will leave. You'll never see me again. I promise."

He chuckles darkly. "It's too late for that. Go take a shower. I'll have someone bring you some clothes. You will eat, then you will tell me everything. Understood?"

He points to the adjoining door that must lead to a bathroom.

"And if I don't?" I meet his eyes.

He smirks. "Test me and see."

Then he strides out of the room.

I wait a couple of minutes to be sure he isn't coming back before I stand, making my way to the bathroom. Once inside, I shut the door and lean against it as I flip the lock.

Turning, I look in the mirror and can't help but cringe. I look like I've been through hell. My hair is a mess. I have blood staining the skin on my neck and hands. Pulling up my borrowed shirt, I see blood stains also on my stomach.

I can't believe I not only passed out, but I slept through someone changing my clothes.

I shiver at the thought. They could have done anything to me.

Mentally, I take inventory of my body. I don't feel like I was violated. Other than my head being sore from where Charles grabbed my hair, my body doesn't even ache too much.

Content with the fact that I seem to be relatively okay, I move to the shower and turn it on. After peeling off the borrowed clothes, I step into the shower. I use his body wash to clean my body quickly. I cringe as I lather in the shampoo, knowing it's going to be a bitch getting the tangles out of my hair without the help of conditioner. Not wanting to be naked for too long, I rush through the shower, wrapping myself in a towel. I consider putting the borrowed clothes back on, but hesitate. He said he was bringing me clothes.

Unlocking the door, I peek my head out into the room.

It's empty.

I rush over to the door, locking it before going to the dresser. I grab another T-shirt and pair of sweats when I hear someone try to open the door. I hear his curse and the sound of keys.

I pull the shirt over my head, glad it falls to my knees, then start to put the sweats on.

When he makes it through the door, his eyes are angry.

"Never lock me out of a room in my own home. Especially when it's my bedroom. Stupid girl."

I bristle at him calling me stupid. "You're an asshole," I mutter under my breath.

He hears me anyway. "If you're going to be brave and say things that will get you killed, at least own it. I am an asshole." He stops, taking in my appearance. "I see you went through my things. Guess you don't need these."

He tosses the clothes he was holding back into the hall onto the floor, making me cringe.

I guess I should have waited for him. The survival side of me is chastising me for being stupid, but that reckless side that just wants life to be over wants to push him.

The survival side wins.

"My apologies, sir." I bow my head, not meeting his eyes.

Maybe if he realizes I'm not a threat to him, he will let me leave. I have nowhere to go, but anywhere would be better than in the belly of the Bratva leader's home. Well, at least now that he knows I'm here. I was fine with it when Ivanna was going to hide me.

"Follow me," he commands.

My heart hammers in my chest. My mind runs through all the potential scenarios. He could be taking me to the front door to kick me out on my ass. He could be leading me to a dark, dingy room or shed to torture me before he kills me. Fuck, he could be escorting me out back to put a bullet in my head.

It's not until we are standing in a dining room that I realize the truth is more unbelievable than anything my mind can come up with.

Instead of doing any of those things, he pulls back a chair, gesturing for me to sit. As soon as I do, he grabs a plate, handing it to me.

"Eat."

He sits at the head of the table, which is the chair to my right. His proximity to me is making me nervous. He makes me uncomfortable.

I peek over at him as he pours a glass of orange juice before setting it in front of me. I couldn't focus on him last night or this morning through my panic, but now that I've calmed a bit, I take him in.

He's gorgeous. His sandy blond hair looks soft. Like I could run my hands through it and it would feel like a cloud. His face is hard, showing his maturity. He's not a boy. No, he is all man. I can see the scruff from a five o'clock shadow on his jaw. His shoulders are broad, his white button-down shirt pulled taut across his chest. He looks like a bodyguard forced to wear business clothes. I wouldn't be surprised if he burst out of that shirt.

He clears his throat, pulling me out of my thoughts. "Fill your plate and eat, Felicity. I won't ask again."

My back stiffens as he uses my name. I didn't tell him it, which begs the question: how did he find out? I wonder if Ivanna told him, but if she did, wouldn't she be here?

When I don't move, he drops his silverware before grabbing my plate, piling food on it. Then he slams it back down in front of me, making me flinch.

"Fucking eat, or do I have to force-feed you too?"

I swallow hard, grabbing my fork. I pick at the eggs, taking small bites while keeping my eyes on him.

He goes back to his own plate, ignoring me.

After a few minutes, he says, "How did you get past my security?"

I shrug.

"When I speak to you, I expect you to use words to speak back," he barks at me. "Tell me how you bypassed my security measures."

I refuse to tattle on Ivanna. If he doesn't know how I got here, maybe he doesn't even know she helped me.

"I saw the wall, and I climbed it. Honestly? I'm not even sure why I came here." I shrug, not meeting his eye.

"Really? So what was your big plan? Was it a suicide mission?" he asks sarcastically.

I shake my head. "It doesn't matter. I didn't mean to impose. Like I told you before, if you let me go, I'll disappear."

"How did you know which room to sneak into? How did you avoid the cameras?"

I let out a deep sigh. "I've been casing the place. How else?"

"Really? So what was the plan?"

"The lights were off, so I figured I would sneak into your room, but I didn't know it was your room. I thought if I could grab a couple of valuables and sneak back out before I got caught, I'd have enough to pawn for a bus ticket out of this place."

His eyes narrow. "So you were planning to steal from the Bratva?"

I shrug. "Not my best plan, but when you're desperate, you do what you have to."

He shakes his head. "You wouldn't be lying to me, would you, *kroshka?*"

I don't recognize the Russian term, but the only Russian Ivanna has taught me are swear words, so that makes sense.

I shake my head. "Never. I know the Bratva kills anyone who crosses them. Especially liars."

He smirks.

A noise behind me startles me. Turning, I see another man walking into the room, followed by Ivanna.

"Lia, you okay?"

She rushes to me, hugging me to her. I don't respond, looking to Nikolai. His face is smug.

He knows everything I just said was a lie.

He's going to kill me.

NIK

The girl in front of me is an enigma. I watch as she wars with herself. I can see her wanting to lash out, showing me that bravery she had last night, but the other part of her wants to survive. That's the part that is being demure.

I know everything she's telling me is a lie. I should be mad, but I'm curious as to why she would lie. She could have thrown Ivanna under the bus, telling me all about their plan. Ivanna already confessed.

So why is she protecting her?

I watch her eyes cut to mine as Ivanna hugs her.

"Have a seat, Ivanna. You too, Dimitri," I say, nodding toward the empty chairs.

Ivanna takes the seat next to Felicity as Dimitri takes the seat on my other side.

"So let's start again, shall we? You were telling me your plans of robbing the place, right?"

Ivanna gasps, turning to Felicity. "Lia, you told him that? He could kill you! Why didn't you tell him the truth?"

Felicity looks at her friend, grabbing her hand. "If I'm already dead for breaking into his room, why would I bring you down with me? You should have pretended not to know me, Ivanna. I don't want you to face the consequences of my decision."

I clear my throat. "Enough. You both are dumber than I thought. Dimitri, what did Anton find at the police station?"

I watch as Felicity tenses. The girl is stupid, but I can't deny that I admire her loyalty.

"The sick fuck is in the hospital. He claims she went crazy and stabbed him for no reason. Someone else saw her in the streets with blood on her and called the police as well. At this point, they know she's here somewhere. Our inside guy bought us time to figure out what we plan to do. If we get rid of her, he will cover for us, but if we plan to leave her alive and let her outside these walls, she will need to make a statement."

Ivanna gasps, gripping Felicity's hand. Felicity keeps her eyes straight ahead, staring at the wall, looking stoic. The only giveaway is the slight tremor in her body.

I stay silent for a moment. "Get the lawyer here to escort Felicity to the police station. She comes back, though. She is not to stay there. Make sure it happens."

Her eyes fly to mine. "You're letting me live?"

"For now. I don't make a habit of killing innocent women." I stand from the table. "Ivanna, put her in the green guest room. As for you"—I turn to her—"finish eating, then stay in your room unless I tell you otherwise. Understood?"

She nods, making me grit my teeth. Reaching down, I grip her chin in my hands. "When I speak, I expect a response."

Her eyes flash with anger before fear wins out. "Understood," she whispers.

"Good. You brought trouble to my door. I will take care of it, but I own you now," I tell her before striding away.

I make my way down the hall into my home office. I don't normally work here, but with the events from last night, I feel I should stay close. I don't trust the girl, especially with Ivy around.

Dimitri follows me into the room, making himself comfortable in one of my guest chairs while I settle behind my desk.

"I'm not going in today. I need you to go take morning reports."

"What are you going to do about the girl? Are you really going to keep her around?" he asks, ignoring what I said.

I huff out a sigh. "Is she eighteen yet?"

"Two more days."

I nod. "Then for two days she stays inside these walls. After that, she's on her own. You know my rules. Normally her punishment would be death for breaking in here, but I think her little stunt is partially a gift as well. She tested our security, and we failed. We have become complacent. So for now, the girl stays. We protect her from that piece of shit and get the charges dropped. Then, in two days she can move on with her life."

"Understood. Rothschild is on the way here to escort her down to the police station."

"Have Maxim go as backup. Send a care package to our favorite detective as well. I want this handled swiftly and quietly."

Without a word, Dimitri stands, turning to leave. Pausing at the door, he turns back to me.

"I hope you know what you're doing, boss."

I wave him off.

Of course I know what I'm doing.

CHAPTER THREE

Lia

Ivanna is excited to have me here in her home, but I can't help but wait for the other shoe to drop.

"Here is the green guest room. I'm down at the other end of the hall. Nik is right across from you."

I swallow hard. I'm not sure it's a good thing that he is keeping me close. Is it because he doesn't trust me? Or is he wanting more than I'm willing to give?

When she opens the door, my eyes widen. No wonder it's called the green room. The entire room is decorated in different shades of green. From the curtains, down to the rug over the hardwood floor.

It's beautiful. Everything looks so expensive. I glance down at my borrowed clothes and can't help but feel unworthy, but at least I'm not dirty.

"What do you think?" Ivanna asks.

"It's beautiful," I say in awe.

She grabs my hand, pulling me farther into the room.

"You have your own private bathroom, too. I'll have Anya bring some of my soaps and stuff in for you. Oh, and I'll get you some clothes too."

I suck in a breath, trying to hold in the sudden emotion that hits me.

I have nothing. Absolutely nothing. Even the clothes on my body belong to someone else. Suddenly, the impact of the last twenty-four hours hits me.

What are you going to do?

"Hey, it's okay, Lia. Everything is going to be okay."

I turn to look at her, tears pricking my eyes.

"Is it really? It doesn't feel that way. I have nothing, Ivanna. Not a single thing to my name. I'm so angry. I couldn't even grab my bag before I had to run off. I mean, how is that fair? Charles tried to molest me, yet I'm the one that lost everything. When does it end?"

Ivanna wraps her arm around me, holding me as I sob.

"It's okay, Lia. We are going to get you some clothes and they will be your clothes. We will get you set up. I won't abandon you," she promises.

"It's not even about the clothes. The only thing I had left of my mother was in that bag. Now it's gone." Pulling back from her, I pull myself together. "I don't need anything else. I refuse to take advantage of your generosity. I appreciate what you and your brother are doing for me, but I think I should just leave. Like he said, I brought trouble to your door."

She shakes her head adamantly. "You don't have that choice anymore. Nik said he was handling it, which means you do what he says now. Trust me, it's for the best. Nik will take care of you."

"For how long, Ivanna? I'm nobody. He's going to get rid of me, eventually. I'm not too sure that I'll be alive when this is all said and done," I say, running my hands through my hair, trying to hide my shaking hands.

She huffs. "Nik is a good man. He won't kill you for no reason. You're talking nonsense. Go get cleaned up. I'll go find you some clothes. We can get you some toiletries later." She turns, slamming the door behind her.

Taking a deep breath, I make my way to the door and open it. I startle when I see a man stationed right outside.

"Close the door," his rough, Russian accent demands.

I do as he says.

She was right. He's not going to let me leave.

After a quick look around the bathroom, I comb my hair with my fingers. The shower this morning was nice, but my hair is a mess now that it has dried. I looked all over for a brush, but it seems there isn't one. I understood what Ivanna said now. All the toiletries in the bathroom seemed geared toward a man. Not that I minded. Beggars can't be choosers.

So far, they have been gracious hosts, allowing me food and comforts. I refuse to complain about any of it.

When I step out of the bathroom, I find an outfit laid out on the bed for me, along with a brush. It's a pair of black slacks and a paisley blouse.

With it, there's a note.

I don't think my bra would fit you, but this should hide the girls well enough. Come downstairs when you are dressed.

-I

Ivanna is built curvier than me. That comes from eating regularly, I suppose. I'm not skin and bones, but I could definitely use a couple more pounds to even out my body. Still, I pull on the slacks, fastening them with the shiny black belt she included. They are a size too big, but they don't look terrible. The blouse is a different story.

Ivanna is blessed in the chest. She can fill out shirts with her large breasts. Not me. Being a measly B cup, I don't have much to covet. It's a good thing in this instance, though. If this shirt fit me the way it was supposed to, I'm sure my nipples would be showing through the silky fabric. Since I'm smaller, it hangs on my frame, giving my girls room to breathe.

It's a little nerve-racking to know I'm about to walk downstairs without a bra on. Opening my door, I find the same man standing outside. This time, he nods and starts walking. I take that as my cue to follow.

Keeping up with his steps the best I can, I walk behind him until he stops outside of a room. He knocks, then opens the door, gesturing for me to go inside.

When I do, I swallow hard.

Three men are in the room. Dimitri, the man from breakfast, Nikolai, and one I've yet to meet. He is dressed in a fancy suit with a briefcase sitting next to him.

"Come in, *kroshka*." At the term, I see Dimitri's eyes widen a little, but he makes no comment.

I make a mental note then to ask Ivanna what that means.

As I draw closer to the desk, Dimitri stands, guiding me to the chair for me to take a seat.

"Hello, Felicity. My name is Daniel Rothschild. I'll be representing you. Before we walk in there, I need to know exactly what happened."

My heart races in my chest. I'm not sure what this is about. I know Nikolai said he would take care of it, but did he mean it?

Probably not. He perhaps said that to appease his sister. They are most likely going to lead me down to the station and hand me over.

Then I'll either go to jail for a long fucking time or they will release me back to Charles. Or maybe send me to a group home. I think I'd prefer the group home.

"Felicity, the man asked you a question," Nikolai's gruff voice demands.

Turning to the man, I answer him, "Why? So you can turn me in?"

He shakes his head, reaching out to touch my hand. I immediately pull back, breathing harder. Nikolai growls, standing from his chair to come around. He kneels before me, placing one hand on my leg.

I jump, but I don't pull back fully. I'm frozen in place as his eyes lock on mine.

"Tell me everything. Don't hold anything back," he commands, jaw clenching.

I take a deep breath, wringing my shaky hands in my lap. Something about his demanding tone has me speaking before I consciously made the decision to do so.

"He's been creepy since the day I moved in. He would stalk my room at night. I had a lock on my door and that worked for a while. Over the past month or so, he has upped his game. Going as far as to whisper through the door at me. I knew he would make a move, so I tried to be as prepared as possible. Last night, he had a key, though. He let himself in and was nice at first." I scoff. "He wanted to coax me into letting him touch me. When I refused, he became angry. He was going to force me. I tried to get away, but he grabbed me by the hair. Before I knew it, he had me beneath him. I refuse to be a victim, so I took my shot and stabbed him and ran."

"Good girl," Nikolai praises me, his thumb drawing circles on my thigh. "What did you stab him with?"

"A switchblade your sister gave me. She showed me how to use it."

"Where is that knife now?" Mr. Rothschild asks, pulling me away from Nikolai's hypnotic gaze.

"Probably in police custody by now. When I stabbed him, I don't really know what happened to it. It might have stayed in his stomach or I might have dropped it, but I didn't have it with me when I was running."

"Then you came here for shelter," Rothschild prods.

"Yes, I came over—"

"He doesn't need those details, *kroshka*." Nik turns to Rothschild, giving him a hard look. "I want that knife back. If it came from Ivanna, then it was one of ours."

"I'll get it. How do you want me to spin this? She has a record in the system for being violent."

Nikolai meets my eyes again. "Why were you so violent?"

"I was trying to survive. Until my last breath, I'll fight anyone who wants to hurt me."

He nods. "Why didn't you go to the police?"

I scoff. "They wouldn't believe me. They never do. Nobody cares what happens to those of us in the system. As far as they are concerned, we're trash."

There's an angry glint in his eye. "That will be taken care of. I promise." He clears his throat, standing. "Here's the story. The man became handsy with her. She was afraid for her life, so she grabbed whatever was close to get him off of her. She doesn't know what it was. After she ran out, she came here because she is friends with my sister, and we took her in. When they ask why you didn't go to them, you tell them the truth. When they ask why we would take you in, you tell them because you are family. Other than that, you don't answer their questions. You need to remain quiet and only answer questions when Rothschild gives you the go-ahead."

"Yes, sir," I murmur, looking down.

His hand comes under my chin, pulling my face up to meet his eyes. "I will take care of this for you. Trust us."

I swallow hard and nod. But for people like me? Trust is hard.

NIK

THE GIRL IS gorgeous. I have to give her that.

When she walked into my office, my dick twitched to life. The outfit was obviously much too large for her, but she still looked good.

When I got close to her, standing over her, I could see right down her shirt, confirming she wasn't wearing a bra.

I had to get them out of here quickly.

"Go with Rothschild. Maxim will go with you two. You'll be safe. We will debrief when you get back," I say as I stand, stepping back.

She stands. "Of course. Thank you." She makes her way out of the room. Rothschild follows her, leaving me and Dimitri.

"She looks lost," he comments.

I don't respond. She does look lost, but she is none of my concern. No matter how much my cock likes her.

"She's a temporary problem. Now that that's handled, let's move onto business."

As I take a seat, there's a knock at the door.

"What?" I bark out.

Ivanna's head pops in. "I want to talk to you."

"Later."

"Please, Nik?" She pouts, pushing her lip out.

Fucking sisters are the worst.

"You have five minutes."

Dimitri moves to retake the chair Felicity vacated while Ivanna takes the seat next to it.

"I want to get Felicity some new clothes. She left all her things behind.

I also wanted to see if you could get her bag back. It has something that's important to her in it."

I scoff. "You want to spend my money to buy the girl clothes *and* you want me to get her things back? Really, Ivy?"

Her turn to scoff. "Don't act like you're so heartless. You didn't shoot her last night and you could have. That has to mean something."

"It means that I do not act rash. I think through my decisions before I carry them out. It has no bearing on my heart. If she walked in right now and I chose to, I would put a bullet in her brain without a second thought. Now if you're done being a petulant child, I have real work to complete."

"Fine. Be the asshole everyone thinks you are. I'll go get her shit myself."

She stands to leave, but before I can stop her, Dimitri does.

"You will not leave this house without me. If you do, you will not enjoy the punishment. Do you understand?" Dimitri hisses.

She grimaces but forces a nod.

It's why I chose Dimitri as her guard. He has been my best friend for most of my life and he's not swayed by my sister's manipulations. It helps that I trust him as much as you can trust another person.

"Good. Get your ass up to your room and finish your fucking homework. Just because I let you stay home today doesn't mean you can slack," Dimitri barks, making her scurry out of the room.

I chuckle. "If anyone else spoke to my sister that way, they'd already be dead."

He grumbles, "It's the only way she listens and does as she's told."

I hold up my hands. "I told you when I gave you the job that however you did it, I didn't care as long as you kept her alive."

"I never should have taken the job," he murmurs to himself.

Changing the subject, I ask, "What about what's going on in Chicago? Any updates?"

"Igor is confirmed dead. They have no proof, but they believe it was the Yakuza. My man on the ground believes that they made a move against the Irish princess who is now with the Yakuza prince. Ivan has fled back to Russia."

I nod. "Any blowback I can expect here?"

He shakes his head. "I've already made it known that we would not be coming to the aid of our brothers in Chicago. After evaluating the situation, I determined it was of the personal nature. The attack was done so after provocation. By doing so, it should keep the Yakuza here calm."

I grunt. I was supposed to go to that fundraiser for the Irish princess. It would have been a good alliance to make, but business here kept me home. Or so that's what I wanted them to believe.

Truth is, I have no desire to find a wife. Ivanna is enough to handle on her own. Adding in another woman who thinks she can manipulate me to get what she wants and I might end up shooting someone. Maybe even the wife.

That's not true. As long as she stayed faithful and loyal, I would never harm the fictional woman, but that's the problem.

I wouldn't be able to trust her. To invite her into my home and trust that she wouldn't put a dagger in my heart the second my eyes close.

It's another reason I need Felicity out of here. I can't trust her either. She's a special kind of dangerous.

Sure, some think danger is someone who is willing to kill, but what is more dangerous is someone who is desperate, reckless.

That's what Felicity is. She had to be to think it was a good idea to sneak into my home.

No matter what Ivanna says, I can't trust the girl.

"Good. Keep an eye on things. Go take morning reports," I demand.

As soon as Dimitri slips out, I stand, putting on my jacket.

I might not like the girl, but there is something I can do for her.

The only kindness she will receive from me.

CHAPTER FOUR

Lia

"Stay in here," Mr. Rothschild says as Maxim puts the car in park. He steps out, briefcase in hand, and approaches a car. I watch as a woman slides out of her car with a folder in hand. The lawyer sets his briefcase on the trunk, opening it. He turns his back toward us so I can't exactly see what's happening, but I watch him take the folder.

"Who's that?"

"Does it matter?" Maxim asks.

"No..." I trail off as Mr. Rothschild turns back toward us, nodding.

"Let's go, Felicity," Maxim says as he slides out of the car.

He opens my door for me, a first.

"Thank you," I say as I get out. "And please, call me Lia."

Wordlessly, he shuts the door and we walk toward Mr. Rothschild. As we approach, he turns, heading toward the building.

Walking into the police station behind Mr. Rothschild is the only thing keeping me from freaking out. The guard at my back doesn't hurt.

When we enter the lobby, we walk right up to the counter.

"Daniel Rothschild here with Felicity Parker to make a formal statement."

The officer looks past him to me. He has a slight sneer on his face, but keeps his mouth closed as he taps a few buttons.

"They are expecting you. I'll lead you back," he says, standing.

As I follow the men, I focus on Mr. Rothschild's back. Nikolai said to trust them. That's a hard thing for me, but I have no other choice. All I can hope is that he means what he said. That I will give a brief statement, then walk back out those doors and back to the safety of his compound.

As much as I don't want to admit it, I do feel safe there. Well, safer than I ever did in Charles's house.

When we round the corner, I glance around Mr. Rothschild, and freeze in my tracks.

My body shakes as I see the man who tried to molest me, sitting in a wheelchair to the side. I take a step back, startling when I run into a broad chest.

I must make a noise because then Mr. Rothschild is turning around to look at me. I can feel my heart beating through my chest and in my temples. My body feels as if I'm frozen in place. All I can do is stare at the man.

He looks up then, smiling at me like he has won. My body feels heavy, like I have a weight on me and my vision tunnels.

"My sweet Felicity."

His voice in my head makes my head dizzy. I feel like I am about to puke.

"W-w-what is he doing here? Shouldn't he be in the hospital?" I choke out.

The man behind me doesn't hesitate. One hand lands on my shoulder, while the other pulls a gun, pointing it at Charles. Several officers jump into action, also pulling their guns.

Mr. Rothschild doesn't even blink. "Everyone put your guns away," he says calmly, as if the scene in front of him isn't happening.

When nobody moves, I shrink back into the man behind me even more.

"It's okay, Felicity. You're safe. He won't touch you with me here," he whispers to me before clearing his throat. "I suggest you make this man disappear before I put a bullet in him. The Bratva does not take kindly to child predators."

I hear a gasp before realizing it came from me.

Everyone is at a standstill until another man steps out of a room.

"What the fuck are you guys doing? This is a police station, not a war zone. Put your fucking guns away," the man demands, shaking his head.

The police officers reluctantly do as he demands, but the man behind me does not.

"Maxim, you too, buddy." The man chuckles.

"When you remove the child predator from Felicity's sight, I will lower my gun. Not a second before," Maxim says, full of disgust.

My anxiety ebbs with the deadly tone Maxim uses. The fact that he is sticking up for me and putting himself in danger so that the man who attacked me cannot harm me makes my heart warm.

"She's the one who attacked me. She needs to be in cuffs," Charles snarls.

"Detective Sanders, you have three seconds before I commit murder," Maxim warns.

The man, or I guess detective, jumps into motion, demanding an officer remove Charles. The entire way out, Charles yells profanities over his shoulder.

I turn, whispering at Maxim, "Aren't they going to arrest you for threatening him?"

He chuckles. "We own the police. Don't worry about it."

"Great. Now that we have that handled, why don't we get this over with." Detective Sanders motions for us to go into the room he came out of.

Mr. Rothschild nods to me, so I follow him into the room. Once I'm in a chair, I look around at the bland room. It's obviously an interrogation room. I smile when I see Maxim post up by the door. He shoots me a wink, making me feel much better about this situation.

"Thank you for coming in today, Ms. Parker. I'm Detective Sanders. I will be taking your statement today. I'm going to record this conversation…" the detective starts.

Mr. Rothschild interrupts him. "Absolutely not. We came down here to make a statement about the abuse Ms. Parker endured last night. We did not agree to recording devices. I'd prefer you accept the written statement that has been prepared."

He opens his briefcase, pulling out a folder. I'm assuming it's the same one he was handed by the woman in the parking lot. She looked like an assistant and now, knowing what she handed him, I'd say I was right. He slides the document across the table toward the detective.

The detective takes a moment to read over the statement. "I will accept this, but I still want to hear it from her."

He slides the paper over, pulling a pen out to hand to me. I reach my hand out to take it, but Mr. Rothschild slaps my hand like a child.

"You take nothing from these people," he hisses at me before handing me a pen from his jacket.

I don't bother reading the document, instead signing where he tells me to. Once done, I hand him his pen back.

"Ask your questions, but no recording devices."

The detective nods. "Felicity, can you walk me through what happened last night?"

So I do. I repeat the story as Nikolai told me, looking to Mr. Rothschild for encouragement when I felt nervous.

He nods every time I do, making me let out a deep breath when I'm done.

"One other question. You said you don't know what you stabbed him with?"

I look at Mr. Rothschild. He nods.

"No idea. I was more focused on him being on top of me and trying to touch me. I just grabbed until my fingers wrapped around something and swung."

He nods. "We are good to go, then. Thank you for coming in, Ms. Parker. We will be in touch."

Mr. Rothschild stands, shaking the man's hand before passing him a sealed, bulky envelope. The detective hands him a smaller envelope before sliding it into his pocket.

"Let's get you back to the house, Felicity," Maxim says, making me stand.

The walk out of the police station is much less eventful. Even so, Maxim stays at my back. His strong demeanor comforting after the events of last night and today. Once we are back in the vehicle, Mr. Rothschild turns to me.

"Everything will be okay now. Keep your mouth shut and go on with your life."

"Wait, what do you mean? Isn't Charles going to be arrested? Won't I have to testify?"

Mr. Rothschild shakes his head. "Nikolai is taking care of everything. You should put this behind you. You'll be eighteen in two days. Start thinking about what you want to do and where you want to go. I suggest as far away from here as possible."

When he turns back, pulling his phone out, I turn and look out the window.

I can't do anything or go anywhere. I have no means to do so, and now that I know Charles isn't even going to face the consequences of his actions, I know I can't stay here.

I'm fucked.

NIK

"Everything is handled. All charges have been dropped. Detective Sanders mentioned that Charles seemed to have some sort of pull, so you may want to look into it. As for the knife, I gave it to Maxim to dispose of," Rothschild says as he stands.

"Great work. Dimitri will settle your bill. Where is Felicity?"

"Maxim said he was escorting her to her room."

"Very good. Thank you for your work."

I shake the man's hand before guiding him to the door. Once he is gone, I leave the room, making my way up to the room she is in.

"How did it go?" I ask Maxim as I approach, wanting confirmation.

"Could have been better, but she seems okay." He shrugs.

"I'll want a full debrief later."

I already heard the story from Rothschild, but he is a lawyer, not a soldier. Maxim is higher on my trust scale than the lawyer.

Without knocking, I open the door to her room. Once inside, I close the door behind me.

Glancing around, I don't see her, but I hear movement from behind the bathroom door.

Stalking over to the door, try the handle, only to find it locked. I barely withhold the growl in the back of my throat as I pound on the door.

"What did I say about locking doors?" I call out to her.

She squeaks a moment before I hear the toilet flush. Then the sink turns on. After nearly a minute, the door opens.

"I had to go to the bathroom. I didn't realize you'd want to watch. You got a thing for golden showers?" she sasses at me.

Fuck if that isn't hot, but I can't think like that. She isn't even eighteen yet. Shit, she's at least seven years younger than me. Unable to think straight, I grip her arm before pushing her into the wall next to the bathroom door. My hand finds its way to her throat as I crowd into her space.

"Watch your tone, little girl. You keep playing with fire and you're going to end up burned."

I can feel her heartbeat pounding furiously under my thumb, but she attempts to save face.

"Maybe I like to burn."

My cock twitches at her admission. She's got guts, that's for sure. As much as I want to explore that, I know I can't. No, I could, but I shouldn't. She has been taken advantage of enough in her life.

I read her file. Her father died from cancer when she was five. Then her mother followed him four years later in a car accident. She went into foster care but acted out against the other children. She jumped from home to home until she ended up here in my town.

It seems Charles likes to take the toughest cases on. Many of his foster children run away close to or after their eighteenth birthday. That's another issue to deal with.

Still, I need to give Felicity what she needs and not take what I want from her. I promised myself I wouldn't be as callous as my father. This is one way I can prove that my rule is different. I will let this girl live. I will send her away and help set her up with a better life. She deserves that much after the loyalty she showed to Ivanna.

I move closer to her face, loving the way her eyes widen and her pulse flutters in my hand.

"Listen closely. I saved your life today only because my sister brought you onto our doorstep. That means your problems became ours. I could have killed you, but I felt merciful and let you live. Do not mistake it as kindness. It wouldn't have been worth the fall back to cover up your murder. You mean nothing to me or to the Bratva. You will stay here for the next two days. Once you turn eighteen, I will place you on a bus and you will leave this city. Then I never want to see you ever again. Is that understood?"

She swallows hard. "Why not let me rot in jail?"

I clench my jaw. How dare she demand answers from me?

Still, I talk before I can stop myself, "I wouldn't give that predator the satisfaction. He would only drop the charges and take custody of you. Then you would disappear."

She takes her lower lip between her teeth, considering her next words.

"I appreciate your help and shelter for the next two days. I'll leave without complaint. Honestly, if you want me to leave right now, I will."

I study her closely for any detection of lies. She seems open and honest, though.

Releasing her throat, I nod as I step back. "I'll allow you to attend school with Ivanna tomorrow if you wish, but you are not required to do so as by Friday you will be on a bus. If you choose to go, Maxim will attend with you. Any other questions?"

She shakes her head.

Without another word, I stalk out of the room, wondering why the hell part of me wants to go back in there and argue with her more.

Why part of me is disappointed that she didn't beg to stay?

An image of the beautiful brunette on her knees begging me flashes behind my eyes, making my dick grow harder.

Fuck. This can't be happening.

Ignoring Maxim, I make my way back to my office.

I can't remember the last time a female even enticed me enough to make my cock twitch. Usually it takes several minutes of attention from their mouth and a concentrated effort to think of anything that actually turns me on before I react, yet with this girl, I'm at full attention after a few words and the image of her on her knees.

"Fuck," I mutter to myself as I slam the door shut, palming my dick to calm it down.

It only strains harder, begging for attention.

I could go find one of the Bratva whores and make them suck me off, but that doesn't sound appealing. The only mouth I want is the pouty one currently living across the hall from my bedroom.

After a moment of hesitation, I lock my office door. Moving back toward my desk, I settle in my chair. Unzipping my pants, I pull my cock out, gripping it hard at the base. Stroking it firmly, I let my head fall back as my eyes close.

All I see are bright blue eyes framed by brown hair. I recall the way her pulse beat against my hand as I held her against the wall. I imagine what she would have done had I claimed her lips, biting and laving at the pillowy goodness.

Would she moan? Press back against me? Beg for more?

I grunt as my pace quickens; the images being the perfect aphrodisiac. Within minutes, I have her on her knees in my head, ready to take the head into her mouth when I blow.

"Fuck," I breathe out as the orgasm hits me harder than anticipated.

My mind is fuzzy for a moment as I feel myself recovering from the sensations.

This girl is going to cause me trouble if I don't get her out of here sooner rather than later.

CHAPTER FIVE

NIK

"What did you decide about the girl?" Dimitri asks the next morning.

I glance into the dining room to see her smiling and laughing with Ivanna. She decided she wanted to go to school today. I think she wants to spend some more time with Ivanna before leaving for good.

I wonder if she told her I was forcing her to leave. I didn't tell her to keep it a secret.

No. She couldn't have told her. I know my feisty ass sister. If Felicity had told her, Ivanna would have already cornered me, cussing me out. She would beg for me to take care of the stray as if she was my responsibility.

I love my sister, but she forgets what my position requires. I need to lead with a lead fist. I can't show vulnerability. Honestly, treating her as well as I do can be viewed as a weakness. It shows that I care for her more than most would. She can be used against me. That's why Dimitri has been her personal bodyguard for the past three years. I needed someone to watch out for her.

Who I knew would put her first, even before me.

"She will be put on a bus tomorrow. Arrange the details. Offer her an envelope of cash to get her started. I don't want her to leave, only to end up dead her first week on the streets. Hopefully, she's smart enough to get set up and spend the money wisely. If not, it will no longer be our problem."

I watch as the girls get up from the table and head out to the main foyer. I lean back against the kitchen counter.

"What about her foster father problem?"

"Have you figured out who his connections are?"

Dimitri shakes his head. "Not yet. I sent Anton to his house, but they've been moved. If he was a low level predator, I don't see how they could have packed up and left so quickly, especially with his injury. Maxim said he couldn't walk. She got him good."

A small smile plays on my face. "Good. Obviously, he has connections. I banned the meat markets, but that doesn't mean they don't still exist elsewhere. Maybe he has connections there? Have Anton check it out."

"Will do. I should go before Ivanna gets it in her head that she can go to school without me."

I chuckle, rubbing my chin. "I don't know why you let her push back so hard."

He laughs. "It's all part of the game. Let her think she has an inch, then snatch it back. Keeps her in line."

"Whatever you say. Let me know when you have an update."

He nods, leaving me in the kitchen alone. I wait several minutes before heading back to my office, making sure to avoid the main foyer. Ever since yesterday, I've been avoiding being too close to her. My body craves her even though it's wrong.

She turns eighteen tomorrow.

I shake my head at the thought. That only means tomorrow, she is gone for good.

Unable to help myself, I glance back toward the front of the house, only to run into something. I reach out, grabbing whatever I hit.

Glancing down, I see the brown head of hair and know it's her.

"I thought you left." I try to maintain a bored voice.

"Sorry. I forgot a sweater. I didn't realize it would be chilly today."

She holds up the dark blue sweater the girl at the store assured me would bring out the color in her eyes.

"Well, you should put it on then," I say, now desperate to see it on her.

I knew it was a bad idea to go pick out her clothes myself. Even worse is the fact that I got that stupid bag back from the police department. They had it in evidence. I left it with Maxim this morning with instructions not to tell her where it came from.

The necklace on her neck proves she received it. It's obviously old, but valuable to her. I knew as soon as I saw it folded up neatly inside a sock that it was important to her.

"Oh. I mean…" she trails off, obviously uncomfortable.

Taking my hands off her arms, I grab the material, holding it out for her to slip into. She turns, giving me her back as she slides it on. Before she can make a move, I pull her hair out from under the collar, letting it fall down her back.

When she turns back, I look right into her eyes. The color really does look deeper when paired with the dark blue.

I should send that assistant a bonus.

Clearing my throat, I give her a curt nod.

"Have a good day at school."

I move past her, determined to get to my office.

Her melodic voice follows me down the hall. "Thanks. You, uh, have a good day doing whatever you do."

Only one more day and she is gone, I remind myself.

Dimitri will put her on the first bus in the morning, knowing I will want her gone sooner rather than later. I contemplated waiting for the day after her birthday. From the files I read, she hasn't had a decent one for a long time. But I can't have temptation under my roof for that long.

It's why I got her bag back for her. While I am ruthless most of the time, I still have a little compassion left inside me. I blame Ivanna for that. After our mother died, my father came at me harder, leaving Ivanna alone.

I would visit her instead, making sure she was being cared for. Her softness helps smooth some of my rough edges. She kept me grounded when Father would have had me go off the deep end.

He always wanted his perfect heir. One without a conscience. He always said women were a distraction only meant to suck your cock when you needed to get off or to use as a pawn.

That's what he wanted for my sister.

My phone ringing brings me out of my thoughts of the past.

"What?" I bark into the phone.

"Nephew. I'm calling to check on you. I heard a rumor that you were mixed up in some police business."

"Uncle Oleg, spying on me again? That could cost you your life," I tease with a hint of an edge.

My uncle Oleg was my father's brother. Not that my father ever gave him any favor based on the blood in their veins. My father was cruel and callous, making him a formidable opponent, but also made him unpopular.

His inability to play the political game ultimately ended his life. No one knows for sure who took his life, but if I had to bet my life savings, I would put it on Uncle Oleg.

He might not have pulled the trigger, but he had a hand in it.

"Of course not. You know I have my birdies out there keeping an ear out for potential issues."

"My apologies for jumping to conclusions. The issue was handled. Was there anything else?"

"Now that you ask, I was hoping you would grace me with your presence tonight at dinner."

I grit my teeth. I hate doing these dinners, but I won't be my father. I will play the political game. While my uncle is under my command, he also has the ear of many influential members of other families. I appease him when I can.

"Where would you like to meet? The steakhouse again?" I ask, mentioning the restaurant we often eat at.

"That would be lovely. Shall I make reservations for more than the two of us for dinner?"

"Yes. I'll bring Ivanna. I know how much you miss her." Lies. He views

Ivanna like my father did, but at least with her there, he won't discuss business.

He pauses. "Very well. See you tonight around seven."

Lia

"What am I doing here, Ivanna?" I whisper as she pulls me forward.

An hour ago, she barged into my room, insisting I get ready quickly. After taking the fastest shower ever, I came out to find her standing at the end of my bed ready to do my hair and makeup. Within forty-five minutes, I was dressed and ready to go. Now I'm standing in front of a fancy restaurant with Maxim at our back while Dimitri leads us.

"It's a dinner. Nikolai invited me out and I told him I wanted you to come too. He didn't argue, so here you are."

I feel uncomfortable. Nikolai hasn't been exactly welcoming since I showed up. I can't help but wait for the other shoe to drop.

The way my body reacted to the feel of him against my skin? That was new.

"Your brother hates me." I twist my hands together as I pause by the opening to the dining room area.

Maxim snorts behind me.

"He doesn't hate you." She pauses, shrugging. "He's just as cuddly as a cactus. You'll get used to it."

Not when he sends me away.

He didn't exactly ask me to keep that a secret, but I did anyway. Ivanna has no idea that he plans to kick me out, most likely today. Maybe that's why he told her I could come. Maybe he will leave me here, in the middle of this restaurant.

"Whatever you say. Let's get this over with," I mumble.

As we make our way closer, I take in the group.

Nikolai is there with another man I don't recognize. This man is older and when he looks at me, I get the chills. My gut wants me to run, but I can't.

The way the man eyes my body makes me tremble and feel dirty. This man looks at me the same way many men have in the past. As if I am a piece of meat for them to devour. I try to shake off my nerves as I approach, but the closer I get, the more I feel uncomfortable.

Nikolai stands as we approach the table. He gives Ivanna a kiss on her temple before turning and pulling me to his side. The shock of the move has me temporarily forgetting about the man across from me.

"Uncle Oleg, this is Felicity, a friend of Ivanna's." Nikolai brings me back to the moment.

Oleg's eyes take in my body once again, making me want to squirm, but I manage to stand still.

The dress is form-fitting, clinging to my body. A little part of me loved that it was so revealing, hoping to entice Nikolai even though I don't want to admit that I'm attracted to him. I'm regretting that now.

"Nice to meet you, Felicity." Oleg's tone is a reflection of his appreciation of my body.

He stands, reaching out his hand to grab mine. I'm about to do the same out of respect when something in the corner catches my attention. It's only a split second, but I know what it is.

A server is standing there, pulling out a gun and pointing it.

Pointing it right at Nikolai.

I don't think. I spin into his chest, attempting to shield his body with my own. The bang sounds out, then my body is propelled forward before a burning sensation is felt in my shoulder. I gasp as my knees collapse, taking Nikolai to the floor with me.

I know that I'm lying on top of him, but I can't move. I can't do anything.

Nikolai rolls me, the jolt from hitting the floor making me cry out. Then his body is over me as bullets fly.

"Find out who the fuck did this," he shouts.

He looks down into my eyes as my vision blurs.

"Nik…"

"Stay still, Felicity," he demands.

"Lia, call me Lia. It hurts," I whisper, tears trailing down my face.

"Shh, *kroshka*. You're going to be okay. I promise."

I vaguely feel him caress my face as my eyes close. "Nik…"

The last thought I have is how beautiful his eyes are as the blackness descends.

CHAPTER SIX

NIK

"Felicity? Lia, stay with me." I tap her cheek, cursing when she doesn't respond. "Fuck."

I look up and find Maxim over us, shooting.

"How many?" I ask.

"Ten total. Three left."

"Take them out quickly. Felicity needs a doctor."

I watch his face tense. I've been having him watch over her for the past two days. Seems she made an impression.

A couple more shots and he makes his move. Within minutes, all that surrounds us is silence.

"Dimitri," I call out.

"Here, boss," he says from a distance.

"Is she hurt?" I call back, asking about Ivanna.

"She's shaken up, but otherwise unharmed."

"Good. Get her out of here."

"What about Felicity?" Ivanna cries out.

"I've got her. Get to safety."

I see movement around me, then I'm left alone with her.

I pull back to look at her. I see the red blooming at her upper left shoulder. I grab each side of my shirt and pull, sending buttons flying as I take it off. Balling it up, I press it to her wound hard.

Everything happened so quickly. One second, I was introducing her. Then she was curling into me. It surprised me until I felt her fall into me the second after I heard the shot.

Did she know it was going to happen, or was she merely seeking comfort from me? I noticed how she reacted to Uncle Oleg. I didn't like the way he was looking at her, either.

Speaking of him. "Maxim?"

"All clear."

"Where is my uncle?"

He pauses, choosing his words carefully. "I don't see him. Must have made it out."

Or he set this up, that distrustful voice in the back of my mind whispers.

"We need to get her out of here. Call the doctor and tell him we are on the way."

I pick Felicity up as carefully as I can, running toward the front of the restaurant. Once there, I slide into the back of the car, keeping her in my lap as I attempt to keep pressure on her wound. Maxim doesn't take it slow, racing to the doctor's house.

Once there, I carry her out of the car and straight into the surgery room the doctor has set up in his home.

"Save her at all costs," I demand, stepping back.

"I'll do what I can," Dr. Daniil promises as he washes his hands.

Then he goes to work with the help of his daughter, his apprentice.

It takes hours, but I don't leave the room. I accept my calls and do whatever I need to, but I can't leave her. I need to know she's okay.

She took a bullet for me.

Why would she do that?

The distrustful side of me wants to believe she knew about the attack. Maybe she was even in on it, but changed her mind at the last second. The other side of me is only worried about her survival. Such a beauty shouldn't be taken from this world too soon.

Finally, the doctor turns and looks at me.

"She lost a lot of blood, but she should be okay. I need to run to the freezer and get some blood for her."

"What's her blood type?"

"O negative."

I step forward, making a fist. "Me too. Use mine."

The doctor looks surprised, but gestures for his daughter to bring a chair closer.

I get it. It's not like someone of my position to offer up his own blood to save another's life. I can't help it though. All I can picture is her beautiful eyes looking into mine with that glassy look. She looked so vulnerable at that moment. It called to a part of me I didn't want to acknowledge, but still. She saved my life. The only reason she wasn't killed immediately is because they were aiming at me. Had she not moved, the bullet would have hit me in the heart.

After several minutes, he has me hooked up, my blood flowing from my veins and into hers.

I sit next to her in silence, my hand holding hers as Maxim quietly speaks to the doctor regarding payment.

At this moment, I don't care.

She took a bullet for me.

Lia

Why does my whole body hurt?

I groan as I try to move. A hand squeezes mine.

"Felicity?"

Peeling my eyes open, I blink up at a form looming over me.

"Ivanna? What's going on?"

"You were shot. Don't you remember?" she says gently.

I try to sit up, but a sharp pain radiates throughout my body, making me cry out as I lie back down and focus on my breathing.

"Hold on. I need to go get Nik."

She rushes away, leaving me to suffer alone.

When I hear the door open again, I turn my head to the side, noticing for the first time that I'm back in my room at their home.

Nikolai strides toward me, worry etched on his face.

"*Kroshka,* how do you feel?"

I swallow hard as his hand reaches out to run a finger down my cheek.

"I feel like I've been hit by a truck."

"More like a bullet. Do you remember anything that happened?"

Closing my eyes, I think back. It's a little fuzzy, but the harder I think, the more I remember.

"We were at a restaurant. Your uncle was giving me the creeps. I saw a server pull out a gun. I stepped in front of you. We fell, but that's all I remember." I lick my lips, my mouth feeling dry.

He grips my hand, sitting on the edge of the bed carefully. Even the slight movement makes me grimace.

"Here, take a drink," he says, grabbing a glass with a straw from the nightstand and holds it in front of me. Taking a drink, I can't help but close my eyes at how good it feels, but I know I need to drink slowly.

"You're saying you stepped in front of me on purpose?" Nikolai asks as he sets the glass back down.

I look up at him. "I did."

He laughs, shaking his head. "You took a bullet for me, *kroshka.* Why?"

I shrug. "I'm not sure I consciously did it. I followed my instinct, which was to protect you for some reason. Maybe it's because of everything you've done for me."

"You almost died." His voice is hard, his face stoic.

My heart stutters. "I feel like I'm half dead now."

His eyes look sad. "You're going to be fine. You've been out for two days, but the doctor assures me you will be okay. The bullet didn't hit anything vital. It'll be like recovering from surgery. In two weeks, you'll feel much better. Another couple after that, you'll be good as new."

"Two weeks? Shouldn't you have dumped me somewhere by now?" I can't hide the bite in my tone, knowing that I should be gone by now.

He shakes his head. "You don't understand what you did. Don't worry, you will. For now, you need to rest up. Maxim will be outside your door, and I'll make sure Ivanna comes and visits often. Here"—he hands me a phone—"if you need anything, call. I put the household staffs' numbers in there." He stands, stepping toward the door.

"Why are you doing this?" I ask, making him pause.

"Rest up and get better. We can talk when you are healed. Maxim will be administering your medication. Don't give him any issues. Maxim," he calls out to the man.

The man pokes his head in, giving me a relieved smile.

"Lia, you're okay. I was worried about you."

Nikolai shoots him a glare, but wipes it away when he turns back to me. "I believe she is due for another pain pill. I'm having soup sent up too. I'll be back to check on her in a little while."

He slips out of the room, leaving Maxim to bring me my medication.

He hands me a small pill and a cold bottle of water.

"So Lia, huh?" I tease him after swallowing the pill.

He shrugs. "You told me to call you that before. After proving what a warrior you are, I think you deserve to be called what you wish. So, Lia it is."

I smile at him. "I don't feel like such a warrior right now."

"You saved the boss's life. Trust me, you are a warrior."

I try to adjust on the bed, but grimace.

"Don't move too much. It's not good for your wound," he reprimands.

I sigh, a little embarrassed. "I have to go to the bathroom."

He nods, taking a step toward me.

"No. You are not going in there with me." I hold out a hand, cursing when pain radiates across my shoulder.

"You really need to not move that arm, Lia. It needs to be in a sling, but you were sleeping, so he left it off. Let me help you put it on."

"Can you get Ivanna? It's nothing personal against you. I just would feel more comfortable with her coming into the bathroom with me."

"Of course. I should have thought of that. Give me a moment." He blushes slightly as he walks away.

He steps out of the room, leaving me to lie back and wait for him to return.

Only a few minutes later, Ivanna comes through the door.

"Sorry, Nik said he needed a minute with you. Asshole didn't come get me when he left. Maxim says you need to go to the bathroom?"

"Yeah. He wanted to go with me, but that's too weird."

She chuckles. "Well, I told him to wait outside the door and listen for us to call out if we need him. Here, he was insistent that you wear this sling if you are moving," she says as she grabs it off the nightstand.

I let her help me into the sling, sitting back once she's done to recover from the energy it took to move.

"This hurts like a motherfucker," I hiss.

Ivanna meets my eyes with tears shimmering in hers. "I'm so glad you're okay. I also need to thank you for saving my brother. I don't know what I would have done if he had died."

My own eyes burn, making me blink rapidly, trying to keep the tears at bay.

"Stop that. It's in the past. Let's focus on the fact that he is alive and well. Now help me to the bathroom."

Slowly, I stand as she holds on to my non-injured arm. I take a couple of steps, but the jolts to my arm are almost unbearable. Add in the pain pill and lack of food for the past two days and I feel dizzy.

"I think we need Maxim to help," Ivanna whispers.

I groan, "I think you're right, but you're undressing me."

"Deal," she says quietly before yelling, "Maxim."

He comes in right away. Seeing our positions, he moves to take Ivanna's spot.

"I got you, Lia."

Maxim takes most of my weight and walks slowly so my shaky legs can keep up. He stops every couple of steps to let me catch my breath. After what feels like forever, we finally step into the bathroom and he leans me against the wall across from the toilet.

"Um..." he says, looking uncomfortable.

"Get out and shut the door. I'll let you know when we need you again," Ivanna says as she pushes him out of the bathroom, making me laugh.

Standing up, I turn, taking two steps back until I feel the front of the toilet at the back of my knees. Slowly, I push my shorts down, trying to keep my breathing even.

"Do you need help?" Ivanna says, watching me.

"I think I got it, but if you could turn around..." I trail off as I grab hold of the counter with my good hand, slowly lowering myself.

"Of course."

Ivanna leans over and turns on the sink, giving me a little privacy before turning to face the door. Once I'm done with my business, I try to stand up but can't. My legs are completely spent.

"Ivanna," I say, getting her attention.

"Need help?" she asks as she shuts off the water, walking toward me.

"Yeah..."

"All good. It's not like you don't have anything I haven't seen before." She winks as she helps me stand, making me laugh.

She helps me pull up my sleep shorts and flushes the toilet for me as I rest my hip on the counter. Once Ivanna's done dressing me, I wash my hand. It's awkward but better than nothing.

"Hey, can I ask you a question?"

"Shoot."

"What does *kroshka* mean?"

"It means baby girl."

"Huh," I mumble, wondering why Nikolai would call me that.

"I honestly don't believe I can make it back to the bed without falling," I say honestly, changing the subject.

"That's okay, that's why we have Maxim." She shrugs, washing her hands.

Once she's done, she opens the door. Maxim turns back toward us with a smile.

"Ready?"

"Yeah," I sigh.

"She can't walk that far again. You'll need to carry her," she tells him.

"Ivanna," I protest weakly.

"As long as you're okay with it, Lia, I have no problem carrying you."

"Fine," I say as he steps forward.

I wrap my good arm around his neck as he puts one arm on my hips and the other below my knees, picking me up bridal style. This time the journey to the bed takes no time at all and when he sets me down, I can't help but fall back into the bed, exhausted.

I hear Ivanna and Maxim talking softly, but I block them out, and let sleep overtake me once more.

"Shh, be quiet. She's still sleeping," someone hisses.

"I am being quiet," another voice mumbles.

Slowly, I open my eyes and can't help but flinch with how bright it is in the room thanks to the open blinds. Turning my head to the other side, I see Ivanna fluttering around the room as Maxim pins a Happy Birthday banner to the wall in front of the bed.

"What are you guys doing?" I rasp, trying to sit up. A radiating pain spreads through my shoulder, making me whimper.

"Hold still," Ivanna chastises as she comes closer.

Once at my side, she helps me move until I'm sitting comfortably.

Sitting up, I can't help but smile at the balloons and decorations around the room. "Thanks. But what's all this?"

"Well, since you were too busy being shot to celebrate your birthday, I thought I would surprise you. What do you think?" Ivanna asks, looking hopeful.

"It looks amazing, thank you." It's been a long time since anyone even acknowledged my birthday.

I look over at the nightstand and see that it's six in the evening.

NIKOLAI

"Dang, I slept the day away."

"You needed it. Now while Maxim steps out to grab my brother and Dimitri, how about you open your present."

"Oh, so I can leave now?" Maxim quips back.

"Shoo," she says, waving him away.

Maxim rolls his eyes at her before looking at me. "I don't know if I said it before, but I'm glad you're okay." He leaves the room before I can formulate a response.

The level of care is touching.

"Now here," Ivanna says as she sets a bag next to my hip on my good side. "I put it in a bag so it would be easy for you to open."

Hesitantly I reach out and grab the tissue paper, pulling it.

"Here, let me pull it out for you."

Ivanna reaches into the bag and removes a brand new backpack.

"I know you wouldn't accept anything crazy from me, so I went with something practical. We both know that your last bag was…" She pauses, trying to choose her words carefully.

"Broken beyond repair?" I deadpan.

"Sure, let's go with that." She nods as she unzips the bag. "I also filled it with a bunch of things you might need and this." She hands me a framed photo of the two of us.

"Thank you," I say, trying to keep the tears at bay as I trail my finger along the frame.

I've never had an actual photo of myself.

"How about we set the picture here for now?" she says as she takes the photo, setting it on the nightstand.

I choke back the tears as Maxim, Dimitri, and Nikolai file into the room.

My heart starts to beat faster as I see them. Part of me still expects Nikolai to kick me out regardless of the gunshot wound.

"I got the cake," Maxim says.

"Bring it over here," Ivanna tells him.

"Is there any way I can get some water?"

Nikolai steps forward, grabbing a pitcher from the table at the side of the room before bringing me the glass. Our fingers brush as he hands it to me, making my hand tingle.

"Thank you," I mumble.

As I take a sip, Dimitri asks, "What are we doing?"

"We are singing Lia happy birthday." Ivanna takes the cake from Maxim, setting it on the tray next to the bed. Once Nikolai takes the empty glass from my hand, Ivanna slides the tray over my lap on the bed, setting the cake up right in front of me.

Dimitri reaches into his pocket and pulls out a lighter and lights the two candles declaring eighteen.

Ivanna starts singing and the guys reluctantly join in.

As messed up as it is, I can't help but love this moment where I've never had one like it.

I know I need to make a wish, but how can I wish for something else when what I have in front of me is more than I've ever really had?

My eyes flicker over to Nikolai for a moment, lighting my blood on fire.

When the song ends, I close my eyes and make a wish I have no business making, blowing out the candles.

Here's to hoping I make it to nineteen.

CHAPTER SEVEN

Lia

Getting better turned into two weeks of being coddled. Ivanna spent all her spare time here with me when she could. She was still going to school and collecting my work. As soon as I could sit up without being in blinding pain, I started working on it. School was always the end goal. Do the best I could and get my diploma so at least I could get a job when I got out of the system.

Maxim has been great as well. He plays cards with me, teaching me to play durak, a popular Russian game. Not only that, but he has been trying to teach me a little Russian as well.

He's a flirt, but I know he doesn't mean it. It's his personality.

I once heard someone say they flirted for sport. Like it was just ingrained in them to act that way toward the other person. That's how I would describe Maxim. He flirts to bring a smile to my face, but I don't feel like he actually likes me as anything more than a friend. Which is fine with me. I don't need that complication.

Then there is Nikolai.

I've only seen him three times since I woke up. The first day when he came to check on me and once more when I tried to leave the house to get fresh air. He came in long enough to chastise me before ordering me to stay in the room until the doctor released me. Whatever doctor that is.

I haven't had the nerve to ask Ivanna or Maxim about him or what his plans for me are. I'm hoping maybe he forgot I was here, and that's why he hasn't been back. That would then mean that maybe I can stay until I'm fully healed and have a plan in place. I'm still not convinced as to his reasoning for keeping me here now. He made it clear before the incident, as I've taken to calling it, that I would be out on my own the day I turned eighteen.

Yet I'm still here.

With Maxim still standing outside my door, I think he probably knows I'm still under his roof. I asked Maxim why he stayed outside my room all the time, but he only responded that it was his job. He wouldn't tell me any more than that.

Still, as I lie here staring at the ceiling, I realize how stir crazy I really am. I'm dying to go outside just so I remember what fresh air smells like.

I glance back at the window. If only it wasn't locked. I attempted to open it a couple of days ago, but the locks wouldn't budge. I feel like a prisoner in here.

A knock on the door brings me out of my depressing thoughts.

"Lia? The doctor is here to see you," Maxim calls through the door.

I jump up, more than ready to meet this mysterious doctor who treated me. I begged to see him so I can get cleared, but Maxim only told me that Nikolai had said it wasn't time.

"Come in," I call out, ready to greet the doctor.

I smile when he steps inside the door behind Maxim. My smile falters when I see Nikolai standing behind him.

"Miss Parker. My name is Dr. Daniil. I'm happy to see you on your feet. How are you feeling?" The older man looks rough around the edges, but his eyes are kind as he looks at me.

I should tell him the truth, but I lie through my teeth, "I feel great. It barely even bothers me anymore. I stopped taking the pain pills four days ago and haven't felt the need for one since."

The doctor gives me a knowing look, but lets it go. "Great. I need to look at the wound. Would you like them to step out? I'll need to lower your shirt on that side to get a better view."

I look down at the T-shirt I'm wearing, well aware that I don't have a bra on underneath it.

"Um, yeah, actually. That would be great."

"No. Maxim can step out, but I'm staying," Nikolai orders from the corner. The doctor startles a little, but nods.

I glare at him. "I don't want you to see me naked, Nikolai. Please leave."

He glances at the doctor. "I don't want to leave you alone with him."

"He's a doctor, for Pete's sake. I'll be fine," I say, rolling my eyes.

"This is not up for negotiation. Maxim, please step out for Felicity's privacy."

Maxim nods, stepping out, closing the door behind him.

I huff in frustration, turning to the doctor.

"Do you mind if I change quickly in the bathroom?"

He nods. "Of course. Take your time."

I shoot another deadly look at Nikolai as I move toward the dresser. I open a drawer and pull out a loose top with an open back to slip on.

It takes me longer to change with my stupid sling, but I eventually manage to get the shirt on even though it leaves me breathless.

When I exit the bathroom, I find Nikolai standing right outside the door in a defensive position, much like Maxim does outside my bedroom door.

Dr. Daniil is paying him no mind, pulling items out of his bag and setting them on the nightstand.

"I'm ready," I tell him, ignoring Nikolai.

Before I can step forward, I feel a warmth at my lower back. Glancing over my shoulder, I meet Nikolai's eyes.

He doesn't speak, but guides me forward with a hand on my lower back, toward the bed. Once near the doctor, I sit down, ignoring the pinch of pain from the movement.

"All right. I'm going to start by listening to your chest and your lungs. Then

I'm going to look at the wound to see how it is healing. The last thing I'll do is take a blood sample and run some tests to make sure everything is good."

"Okay. If everything is good, I can move around more? Go outside and maybe go back to school?"

Dr. Daniil looks surprised, meeting Nikolai's eyes as he stands next to me.

"We can discuss that," he mumbles, fumbling with his stethoscope.

I eye Nikolai, seeing his face set in a cold, impassive manner.

So maybe it wasn't the good doctor's orders to keep me locked up. Maybe it was Nikolai's. Why would he want to keep me prisoner here, though? He wanted me gone before.

I let the doctor move through his routine. I didn't miss the way Nikolai tensed every time the doctor touched me. Nor did I miss the way he moved closer when he pulled the left side of my shirt down to inspect my wound.

Dr. Daniil remained professional, but the way Nikolai was glaring at him by the end of the visit, you would have thought he did something wrong.

"I think you are healing quite well. Finish the antibiotics I prescribed. If you need the pain pills, use them. Don't try to be strong and refuse them out of pride. The more relaxed you are, the less chance you will reinjure yourself."

"Thank you," I tell him, then decide to test him. "I can go back to school now, right?"

Instead of looking at the doctor, I glance over at Nikolai, catching the shake of his head.

"Never mind, Doctor. Thank you for coming here. That will be all," I dismiss the man, my eyes locked on the side of Nikolai's face.

"I'll walk you out," Nikolai states.

"No, you won't. You're going to tell me why you have me locked up here like a prisoner."

Nikolai brings his eyes to mine. "You don't command me, little girl."

"Leave, Dr. Daniil," I command.

The doctor hesitates, but I hear him open the door and leave the room. As soon as the door closes behind him, I step into Nikolai.

"I'm not your prisoner. I will not be holed up in this room any longer. The doctor says I'm healing well. I will leave this room."

He looks like he wants to argue, but takes a deep breath.

"I'll allow you to roam the grounds with Maxim as your escort. No school. Not until the sling comes off."

"That's ridiculous. I want to go back to school." I shake my head.

"Don't take my kindness for granted. I don't have to let you do anything. You are living in my home. You are under my protection. That makes you mine to do with as I please. Now, I see how you desire some freedom, so I am compromising. Something that I never do with anyone ever, so take the win and say thank you."

I swallow hard at the vehemence in his tone. He sounds like he is barely controlling his rage.

Not willing to rattle his cage, I take his advice and accept the win.

"Thank you. I want to eat my meals downstairs from now on too. Will that be allowed?" I ask softly.

He gives me a curt nod. "You can move about the house as you see fit, but if you injure yourself even once, it's back to this room. Understood?"

I let out a deep sigh. "Fine, but I need a laptop and I want to have contact with my teachers. I don't want to fall behind because of this."

"I'll arrange it. Now, if you are done, I need to get back to work."

As he moves toward the door, I call out to him, "Nikolai."

He looks at me over his shoulder, but doesn't speak.

"Why am I still here?"

"I changed my mind. I'm not ready to let you leave yet."

Before I can respond, he is out the door. Leaving me to wonder what that means.

NIK

"She can leave her room and go outside, but not outside our walls," I tell Maxim after I exit the room.

"Got it," he replies, keeping his watch outside the door.

"You're doing a great job," I tell him.

He chuckles. "It's not like she does much."

"I know, but still."

He doesn't understand, but I feel it's important to tell your men when they do well. My father never did. He only ever spoke to his men when they fucked up. It bred a lot of anger in the ranks. Honestly, it might be why he ended up dead at the end of the day.

No one got it worse than me. My father never once told me he was proud of me or praised me for doing anything right. He only ever hit and abused me when I did something wrong.

Thankfully, his physical mistreatments ended with me. Ivanna was only ever ignored. She was his chess piece to move on the board in the form of marriage. As soon as he died, I made it known that Ivanna would not be married off for political gain.

I would allow her a choice. I mean, I still have to approve of the poor bastard, but I would allow her a choice.

That's why I treat my men so well. Why I give them praise and remind them they are appreciated. An empire is only as good as its inhabitants. If my men are dissatisfied, they may want to end my reign. They may have feared my father, but they were never truly loyal to him.

I want my men to choose to be loyal to me. Men who are dedicated out of fear can be bought or swayed. Men who are steadfast out of mutual respect will be less likely to be turned away from that loyalty.

Entering my office, I smile when I find Dimitri.

"You're home early. Ivanna cut class again?"

He shakes his head. "She heard the doctor was coming and wanted to check on Felicity. Ivanna's hoping she can go back to school with her. She even convinced the front office to switch her schedule so she will be in all the same classes as Felicity. This friendship is getting out of hand."

I shrug. "I don't mind. Felicity isn't a danger to us or the Bratva. If Ivanna wants to keep her as a friend, I approve."

He chuckles, smirking. "I'm sure you do. So how is your little pet, anyway?"

I shoot a glare at him. "She is not my pet. I'm only caring for her as if she were one of the men."

"Sure," he drawls. "I'm sure if Maxim had taken a bullet for you, you would have carried him to the doctor yourself, offering your blood to save his very existence. Then let him sleep in the room across from yours so you can stalk him at night."

I grimace at his words. He knows more than he should.

"Are you spying on me, Dimitri?"

He laughs harder. "No, but I don't need to. I know you. There is no way that girl sleeps across the hall and you don't sneak in to check on her at least four times a night. You're obsessed."

"Not obsessed. Concerned. She took a bullet meant to kill me. I feel I owe her some sort of concern."

"Sure. It has nothing to do with the fact that she is hot as sin and isn't afraid to speak up to you. I misunderstood."

"You're treading a thin line, my friend."

He lets out a sigh. "I'm pointing out how it looks. If you keep catering to her like this, you will be announcing to anyone around that you care about her. Are you ready for the target that will paint on her back?"

"I'll handle it."

"Oh, so you are aware? Because I know for a fact that if I was the person who was trying to kill you, I would add her to the hit list for thwarting my plans."

"Oleg was involved," I tell him, finally voicing what I have known for weeks.

"What? When did you find out?"

I shake my head. "I don't know for sure. He had no idea that Felicity would be there. Did you see how he stood to greet her? At the time, I thought it was because he was leering at her, but the more I think about it, it is odd. He never stands to greet those he feels are lesser than him. There is no way he views Felicity as anything more than a hot body. That means he was trying to distract her and get her away from me. Had she leaned across the table to shake his hand instead of curling into me, I would be dead right now."

"Well damn. You're right. It makes sense. I was more focused on Ivanna to even consider his positioning. Honestly, none of the bullets came his way at all. Ours either. They were focused on you."

"Exactly. I want eyes on him. Who do we have that can be trusted? He still has friends within my ranks."

"I'll put Alexei on it. He's a recluse and sticks to his computers, so he will be the best to be covert. That, and I brought him in. Saved his life. His loyalty is to me even over you, sorry to say, boss."

I nod. "Your loyalty is to me, so that means his is as well. Put him on it and pay him double for it. I want answers as quickly as possible."

"On it. Anything else?"

"No. Keep an ear to the ground. I can feel something brewing and it's going to get ugly fast."

"Will do, boss."

As Dimitri stands to leave, I pull up my phone to check the security cameras. It only takes a couple of seconds to find her.

The brown-haired beauty standing in the middle of the garden Ivanna and my mother planted when they were young.

God, she's beautiful.

CHAPTER EIGHT

Lia

Gasping awake, I clutch at my chest.

A glint of light shining through the window has me jumping to attention. I scramble out of bed and toward the window to look out.

It's dark out, but I can see a figure standing near a tree by the wall. Another light glints, shining into the room.

Gasping, I jump back, pressing myself to the wall. After a moment, my mind clears. I run toward the door, to my guard.

Swinging it open, I panic.

Maxim isn't there.

Fuck.

Running across the hall, I slip into Nikolai's room.

"Nik," I hiss.

He sits up in an instant, swinging his legs out of the bed.

"What is it, *kroshka*? What happened?" he rasps.

My heart is hammering in my chest. I can't even enjoy the view of him shirtless, in only a pair of boxers.

"I think I saw something outside my window and Maxim isn't outside my door."

Grabbing his phone off the nightstand, bringing it to his ear. He strides toward me and pulls me into his chest.

"Secure the property, especially Felicity's room. Possible breach."

Pulling me farther into the room, he sets the phone back down on the nightstand and pushes me onto the bed before moving toward his closet.

"Do you think Maxim is okay?" I whisper, tears filling my eyes at the thought of anything happening to him.

He steps back out to stand in front of me with clothes in his hand.

"He's fine. He was sleeping. You think he sits outside your room twenty-four-seven?" Nikolai's tone is harsh.

He steps away from me, pulling on a pair of pants and a shirt.

"I guess I never thought about it," I admit, looking to the ground.

I did always assume someone was outside my door. I've never opened it and not seen Maxim, but I have never had a reason to leave so late.

A loud noise jolts me from my thoughts. I glance over toward the closet Nikolai disappeared into. After a moment, Nikolai comes back to me, pushing something over my head. Then I hear him attach Velcro straps.

The movement hurts my still healing shoulder, but I let him do whatever he needs to.

Then he steps back, observing me.

"Come with me, Lia," he says softly, holding his hand out to me.

Placing my hand in his hand, he pulls me behind him.

"Stay close to me," he whispers, pulling a gun out of his waistband.

Then he's on the move. I clutch at his back while his hand stays in mine.

We wind through the house until we are in a library. Once there, he moves to a painting, pushing it aside to show a keypad. He types in a number, then presses his thumb to it.

There's a whoosh sound, then a bookcase next to us opens. He ushers me through the opening, stopping when he sees Dimitri and Ivanna.

"Stay with the girls," he barks at Dimitri.

Then he turns to me, pressing a kiss to my temple, surprising me with the gentle show of affection.

"Stay in here with Dimitri. He will keep you safe."

I wanted to beg him to stay with me, but I didn't. While I knew logically I was safe with Dimitri, I only ever felt safe with Nikolai around.

Instead of giving in to my internal need, I stepped back as he exited the room. Then Dimitri pressed a button, the door closing behind him.

Whirling, I face Dimitri and Ivanna. Ivanna looks pissed. Glancing over to Dimitri, I see scratch marks on his face.

"What happened? Did you run into someone?"

What if someone is in the house and Nikolai just ran out there to face them? What if he gets hurt? My mind is racing with the possibilities.

Ivanna chuckles, coming to grab my hand.

"Yeah. Me. He pulled me out of bed from a dead sleep. He should have known better," she says, calming me instantly.

Dimitri scoffs. "I tried waking you. It's not my fault you sleep like the dead. I had to act. There is a threat."

She rolls her eyes at him before looking back to the wall of screens. "There is no threat."

Turning, I glance at the monitors as well, my heart catching when I see Nikolai among his men clearing the house.

"I saw someone outside my window. Whoever it was shined something in my window," I tell her, unable to take my eyes away from the screen.

"Are you sure it wasn't a guard? Maybe they weren't shining it at you, but in general?"

I bite my lip, feeling a little foolish. Could it have been? It's not like I took extra time to study the figure.

"It could have been, I guess. It seemed like they were inside the walls. I swear I saw someone standing by the tree I can see from my window." I turn, eyes wide on Dimitri. "You guys would know if someone got inside, right?"

He gives me what I think is supposed to be a comforting smile.

"Of course. You're perfectly safe," he says, trying to pacify me.

I scoff sarcastically. "Sure. I'm safe and sound here in this wonderful safe room. What about Nikolai? Or Maxim? Are they safe too?"

Dimitri busts out laughing. "You're worried about them? You do realize Nik is the leader of the California chapter of the Bratva and Maxim is one of his top enforcers, right? They can handle themselves."

I narrow my eyes on him, putting my hand over my wound. "Yeah, and it wasn't like Nikolai almost got shot oh say two weeks ago, right? Let's just pretend you're all invincible."

"He's going to love this," Dimitri mutters under his breath.

Ivanna smacks him on the back of the head, making him grunt.

"Be nice. Lia isn't used to this lifestyle like we are. You're being an ass," she scolds.

He steps closer to her. "Hit me again and I'll—"

"You'll what?" Ivanna cuts him off, getting right up into his face. "Finish that sentence. I dare you."

They have a little stare down, the tension in the air thick enough to choke me. The anger mixed with sexual tension is too much for me.

I turn away, feeling uncomfortable with their little game. Instead, I focus back on the screens.

My eyes find Maxim, who is now stationed in the room outside the safe room I'm in. I want to open the door and ask him what's going on, but Dimitri would never let me. Besides, I don't even know how.

I hear Ivanna and Dimitri bickering behind me, but my eyes are drawn to Nikolai as he searches the yard. The way he moves is graceful yet deadly. When he slips out of the frame, my heart pounds harder.

After a few moments, I hear Dimitri's phone ring.

"Boss," he answers.

I spin, staring at him. He listens intently before hanging up the phone.

"What's wrong?" I demand.

Dimitri smiles. "Everything is clear. Nothing suspicious. He wants Maxim to bring you outside so you can point out where you think you saw the person. I'm to take Ivanna to bed."

"Like you could get someone of my caliber in bed," she says lightly.

"That's not what I meant," he growls.

Ivanna ignores him, walking to the door to press some buttons on the keypad. The door opens, and she stalks out.

She stops at the door to turn toward me. "Do you need backup?"

"I have Maxim. I appreciate it though," I say, pointing at the man.

She gives me a smile. "You know where I'll be if you change your mind."

"Thanks."

As she leaves, Dimitri trails behind her, looking frustrated. I don't know what is up with them, but it's going to explode at some point. I don't want to be anywhere near any of that.

"Lia, you ready to go? Oh, you need shoes," Maxim says, his eyes meeting my feet.

I must look like a mess in my sleep shorts and a tank top under the bulletproof vest strapped to my chest.

"I can slip on a pair at the door," I tell him, letting him lead me from the room.

He nods, his eyes still continually scanning the room for threats. It makes me take a step closer to him, my own eyes traveling around the house I've come to think of as home.

"I thought it was clear?" I whisper to him.

He startles, looking down at me. "It is. Sorry, I am being cautious. You are perfectly safe, Lia."

I give him a small smile, but I don't feel safe.

At the front door, I open the closet door, slipping on a pair of flip-flops I stored here. Then I follow Maxim out the door.

I shiver a little at the chill of the breeze, but continue to follow him as he leads me around the house toward the area of the estate that my window faces. My body finally relaxes a little when I see Nikolai standing there, his eyes taking in his surroundings.

"Boss," Maxim greets.

"Thank you. Give us a minute, but don't go far," Nikolai orders.

Maxim retreats the way we came, but stops at the corner of the house.

"Lia, where did you see this figure?" Nikolai asks, stepping closer to me.

I glance over the yard, trying to see which tree it was from my room. I take a step forward, but Nikolai places a hand on my arm, causing me to freeze.

"Don't go over there, just point it out. I'll check it out."

I turn back to him and nod.

"I think it was that tree there by the wall. They were standing to the right of it, almost like they were leaning on it."

"You said they shined something in your window?"

"Yeah. It's what woke me up. I can't stand light while I'm trying to sleep. When I glanced out to see what it was, I saw the figure, but they shined it again before I could get a good look."

"Alright. I'll check it out. Go back inside with Maxim," he demands as he presses a hand to my lower back, urging me toward the guard.

I stop, turning. "No. I don't want to be kept in a bubble. I want to know what is going on."

"Lia, this isn't the time. Go inside where it's safe."

Crossing my arms over my chest, I pop my hip. "I thought it was all clear. Isn't that why I'm out here and not in the safe room? I'm staying. You can't make me leave."

He growls, "You will do as I say. Now go inside."

"You don't command me, Nikolai. I'm not one of your soldiers. Honestly, I'm nothing more than a passing guest. Isn't that what you told me once?"

Something flashes in his eyes. "That was before. Now get your ass in the house."

"No."

His eyes flare before he steps forward. "I don't want to hurt you, but if you don't go in the house, I will pick your ass up and carry you in there myself."

I narrow my eyes. "Touch me and I'll kick your ass."

He chuckles, rubbing his chin. "Is that your final answer?"

Before I can even respond, he steps toward me, carefully, but quickly placing his shoulder into my stomach to place me over his shoulder.

"Nikolai, damn it, let me down," I scream.

I go to hit his back, but the new position strains my still healing arm.

"Ow," I curse.

He immediately stops, placing me back on the ground. Gently, he grabs my shoulder to look at it.

"I'm fine," I hiss, pulling back.

His eyes harden. "In the house or back up you go. Those are your two options."

I glare at him. "To think I was worried about you, asshole," I mutter under my breath.

"What was that?" he asks, a quirk in his eyebrow.

I give him a mocking curtsy. "Yes, master. I shall go back to the house with the womenfolk while you men secure the scene since I am useless."

"*Kroshka...*" he starts to say.

"No. I get it. Helpless female here. Go on and do whatever you do. I'm going to bed."

I turn before he can respond, marching back into the house, Maxim hot on my trail.

"He only wants you to be safe, Lia," Maxim says quietly.

I stop before my door, turning toward him. "That's admirable, but at the same time, it is not his job to tend to my safety. Unless he locks me in a padded room, there is no way to guarantee that I will always be safe and unharmed. If he did, what kind of life would that be? I can take care of myself. I don't need someone trying to control me. Honestly, I think it's about time I pack my shit and move on."

"Don't act rash. You're upset, but this place is good for you. Ivanna loves you and the boss cares."

I turn back to him, understanding what he's trying to say delicately. I'm being irrational. Wanting to run at the first sign of trouble. It's my MO. Cut the strings before they grow too attached.

I let out a deep sigh, bone tired. "I just want to go to sleep. Not that I think I will get much with the way I woke up. I promise I won't make any decisions until I have a clear mind."

"Good. Go try to sleep. I'll stay outside your door to keep you safe."

A pinch of guilt hits me when I remember Nikolai telling me he had been in bed. I can't let him give up his sleep to watch over me.

"It's okay, Maxim. I'm safe here. I know that. I don't need you to stand guard."

He chuckles. "It wasn't an offer, not that I wouldn't offer to protect you. It's an order from the big man himself. I'll be here until he concludes his investigation."

"Very well," I say. "Good night."

"Good night. Sleep well."

Shutting the door behind me, I pull on the Velcro straps, keeping the bulletproof vest on my chest. Finally getting it off, I realize how tight it had actually been. I'm finally able to take a full breath. Making my way over to my window, I glance out.

My heart kicks up like it always does when I see Nikolai. He's talking to Dimitri over by the tree I had pointed out, but up here, I realize it's the wrong tree.

"Maxim," I call out.

He opens the door, concern on his face.

"I was wrong. It wasn't the tree they are at. It was the one to the left a couple hundred feet."

Maxim pulls out his phone. I watch as Nikolai answers.

"She's fine. She said the tree is actually a couple hundred feet to the left."

Nikolai looks up at my window, spotting me standing there. He moves, but I realize he thought I meant his left.

"No, the other way," I tell Maxim.

He repeats my words until Nikolai is standing at the correct tree.

My body shivers when I see him standing in the exact spot as the figure before. Without lights, I can't make out his face. It's almost as if he was the figure, even though I know that is illogical.

"Lia, boss wants to talk to you."

Maxim holds out his phone. I take it, pressing it to my ear.

"Go to sleep, *kroshka*. I'll come see you when I'm done."

"You'll tell me what you found?" I phrase it as a question, but I am not really asking.

He sighs. "Yes. Go to sleep. I will see you soon."

"Okay." I pause, the phone still to my ear. I can feel his eyes on me.

"Be safe," I whisper after a moment of silence before ending the call. Turning, I hand it back to Maxim, giving him a small smile.

"Thank you."

"Of course."

As he leaves, I slide into bed, knowing very well that I won't be sleeping. Not until I know Nikolai is inside and safe.

NIK

"She's got you by the balls, man," Dimitri teases.

"It's not like that." I shake my head in denial.

"Oh really? *Kroshka?* You never give people pet names."

"Enough. She said this is where she saw the person."

"You believe her? What if she was having a nightmare?"

I ignore him, searching around the tree and on the ground. It only takes a few moments for me to find it.

A photo of me from the restaurant with a knife in the middle as it's stabbed into the ground. It's a clear sign.

"Check the cameras. Get some gloves. I want this tested for fingerprints. Someone was here, and they were sending a message. I think they targeted her room because she stepped in the way," I say, looking at Dimitri.

His face has lost all humor as he looks at the photo.

"How did they get on our property without tripping the new security I put in place?"

I shake my head. "No idea. You need to figure it out, though. This can't happen again. I won't allow it."

He grimaces. "Are you sure they were targeting her? If they knew she was in that room, that means they have inside information."

I had already drawn the conclusion he is now coming to. Inside information means at least one of my men is compromised. I'll need to take a closer look at all the men who have been on the grounds since she came here. It will be tedious, but I cannot have a traitor among us.

"Get the cameras. Maxim is outside Lia's room. I am going to check him out first, although I feel he is loyal. I just need to be absolutely sure. We need to get together a small group of men we know are loyal to help protect the girls. From now on, someone is always on them. We will put a cot in Ivanna's room for you to sleep on. I'll stay with Lia. They are not to be alone at all."

"Are you sure we need to go to this extreme?"

I look back down at the photo.

"They've already made one move against me. We still have no leads as to who it was, either. They were able to get on our property without us knowing. What if they had gotten into the house? Hurt Ivanna or Lia? No, this is necessary."

I watch as the realization passes through his eyes. He would die for my sister. It's why I assigned him as her personal guard, even though he is my second. I wouldn't trust her with anyone else.

"Understood. I'll get this all situated then take my post."

"Thanks. I'm going to go check Maxim's background again to see if I missed anything so I can clear him quickly. Then I'm going to stay with Lia for the rest of the night. Tomorrow, we will start combing through each and every one of our men. I will not rest until the rat is found."

"We will catch him and show him what we do to rats," Dimitri lets out a disgusted sound.

Pulling out a pair of gloves from his pocket, he leans down and carefully picks up the photo and knife.

"You had those in your pocket?" I ask, curious.

"Always be prepared, right?" He chuckles as he walks away.

I make my way inside. Going to my office, I pull out my personal laptop. I bring up Maxim's file along with the camera feeds from the staff quarters. Not all my guards stay on site, but Maxim does. I watch as he walks into his room shortly after ten in the evening. That's about the time I went to bed, relieving him of his duty.

His door shuts and stays closed. I fast forward, noting when it opens again. Two forty-three a.m. Only a minute after the house was put on lockdown.

That doesn't clear him. He could have left through his window, but that's easy enough to check. Pulling up my security system, I see his window sensor hasn't been opened in months. Pulling the outside camera to be sure, I watch, happy to not find him in the footage.

I glance through his file again. Maxim is one of my best men. I recruited him young. Born to a junkie mother, he never knew his father. He was getting into fights in school and causing trouble. Detective Sanders called me, giving me the lowdown on him after one fight went too far. He stabbed a kid twice his age and size and ended up in jail.

I went to see him. He was tough. Not willing to even look at me. He refused to answer my questions or even tell me his name.

So I bailed him out. Then I brought him home and gave him the room he's in now. Father wasn't happy about it, but I labeled him my progeny, so he allowed it. I taught him everything he knows. It's why I wasn't overly concerned with him being the culprit.

Better safe than sorry.

Once my mind is settled, I lock everything up. As soon as I approach Lia's room, I give Maxim a nod.

"Good job out there. From now on, Lia's not to be left alone. I'll give you more details tomorrow, but know that she is the number one priority for you. Dimitri will protect Ivanna."

"It's my pleasure." He bows his head, a formal sign of respect.

Even though I trust him with Lia's life, the warm tone of his voice grates on my nerves. He shouldn't care for her. She's not his to do so with. Not that she's mine either, but Lia doesn't need to be with Maxim. He is almost as bad as I am. I'll need to keep an eye on that.

"Great. You're dismissed for the night. I'll be staying with her," I tell him coolly.

"Call me when you need me back up here," he says before turning to leave.

I feel a pinch of guilt for the rude way I spoke to him, but I can't bring myself to care. I need to look in on Lia and make sure she's safe and unharmed. I don't even know why.

It's like she calls to the protector in me that desires a woman I can take care of. That I can care for and look after. Except she's more than that. When she spoke back to me in the yard? That had my dick growing hard, even though it also pissed me off. She has me questioning my sanity. How can I find this young woman sexy and alluring? Fuck, she's the same age as my sister.

Yet, it doesn't stop me from stepping into her room. Or walking to her bed. When I find her eyes open and on me, it doesn't stop me from sitting beside her and brushing back her hair.

I can't control myself around her, but I'm not sure I want to.

"What happened?" she whispers as if the quiet in the room would be disturbed if she spoke too loud.

I hesitate, knowing I should lie, but when I see her bandaged arm, I change my mind. I should be wary to trust her, but that mark will forever remind me she stepped between me and a bullet when she didn't have to.

"We found something. We don't know who it was, but we are working on it. In the meantime, I need you to allow Maxim to keep a closer eye on you. You can trust him to protect you along with Dimitri, but don't trust anyone else."

Her eyes grow wide. "You think someone who works for you did it?"

I shake my head. "I can't say anything for sure, but I am erring on the side of caution for now."

She swallows hard. "Okay. I can do that, but when will he sleep? He can't stay outside my door forever."

I smile. "I'll be taking the night watch."

She lets out a relieved sigh. "That makes sense since you are across the hall. I guess you have been doing that anyway, huh?"

I shrug. "Before, Maxim was there to help you while you were awake to make sure you didn't harm yourself by trying to get anything you needed. Now he is there solely for your protection. You didn't really need protection while you slept before. Now that you do, I will watch over you. I'll sleep on the couch."

Her eyes startle. "The couch? What? You're staying in here?"

"It's the best way to protect you. I'm a light sleeper, as you have found out not once, but twice now. You'll be perfectly safe with me."

She bites her bottom lip. "I should take the couch. I'm smaller. You need more room."

"You need the comfort more than me. That couch is not the worst place I've ever slept."

It's the truth too. My father used to throw me in the cells when I disappointed him. The rats crawling over me while I recovered from my latest beating was nightmare-inducing terror, yet I survived. It made me stronger.

"If you insist on sleeping in here, the least you can do is sleep in the bed, Nikolai. I won't be able to sleep knowing you are uncomfortable on the couch."

I shake my head. "This isn't a negotiation. You will sleep in this bed."

She huffs, "Fine, but only if you will be also sleeping in this bed too. There's plenty of room for two. You can stay on your side while I stay on mine."

I pause. This is a bad idea. A really fucking bad idea, yet that internal alarm that should be blaring is oddly silent.

"Fine. Don't molest me in my sleep," I mutter, moving to the other side of the bed to undress. I remove the Glock from my waistband, placing it on the nightstand. Next is my phone. Then I pull my shirt over my head, tossing it on the armchair next to the window. As I undo my pants, I reconsider my position.

"You have to move to this side. I need to sleep by the door."

She grunts, "I always sleep here."

"Not anymore. Move over."

I toss my pants onto the chair, leaving me in my boxers. I grab the gun and phone, making my way to the other side to place them on the nightstand she was using.

"No way. You can get over it."

I try to withhold it, but a growl sneaks out.

"Stop growling at me." She sounds frustrated.

"Listen to reason then. What happens if someone comes through the door? If I sleep by the door, they will get to me first. It's a protective measure for you."

She bites that lip again, the moonlight highlighting her features in the dark. Finally, she moves over, opening the blanket for me to slide inside.

"Thank you," I tell her as I take her place, the smell of her overwhelming me along with the heat she left behind.

"Don't get used to it. I can understand your logic, which is the only reason I agreed. You can't keep commanding me to do what you want."

I smile to myself. "Of course. Sleep well, *kroshka*."

She mumbles something under her breath before speaking louder, "Good night, Nikolai. You better not snore."

I don't respond, instead content to lie in bed with her listening as her breathing evens out until she is finally asleep.

"You'll learn that my word is law one day, *kroshka,* and I'll enjoy every second teaching you it," I whisper into the dark with a smile on my face.

CHAPTER NINE

Lia

I wake in the morning with the sun shining on my face. I never closed the blinds last night after everything.

That's when it comes back to me. Nikolai sliding into bed beside me. I didn't think I'd be able to fall asleep with him so close and so naked, but the next thing I knew, I was out. The way I feel around him is a conundrum.

Sometimes, I'm so pissed at him I could punch him, but then the next second I want to climb him like a tree. One thing that never changes, though, is the way I feel safe around him. Even when I've pushed back against him, he has never made any attempt to harm me. If anything, he's a little too protective of me.

Turning over slowly, I crack my eyes open to take in his side of the bed. I let out a heavy sigh when I realize he is gone. Reaching over, I find his side of the bed cold, letting me know he's been gone for a while now.

I was not ready to face him this morning. Slipping out of bed, I take in the outfit I wore last night. A pair of shorts and a tight tank. My cheeks heat at the thought of him lying next to me while I was dressed in barely anything.

My mind starts to wander to the things he could have done to me. The way his hand would have slipped across my stomach. How it would have been so easy for him to pick a direction, slipping up under my tank to caress my breasts or down under my shorts toward my heated center.

I clench my legs together, thinking about it.

It's right then that the door opens, making me shriek.

Breathing hard, I glance up at Nikolai standing there looking like a damn god.

"Are you okay?" he asks, his eyes taking in my body.

I don't miss the heat behind his eyes as he takes me in. My nipples are hard, which he hones right in on.

"I'm fine," I tell him, crossing my arms over my chest.

"Maybe you need a hot shower. You seem cold." The small smirk on his face tells me he knows I'm not cold.

"Great idea. You can go now."

He laughs. "Breakfast will be ready in twenty minutes. I expect you in the dining room."

"Yes sir," I sass.

His grin only grows. "I could get used to you calling me sir."

Fuck. That only makes my legs clench harder. Especially in that dark, gravelly voice of his.

I'm in so much trouble.

"You have nineteen minutes now. Shower, *kroshka*."

As soon as the door shuts behind him, I hustle my way into the bathroom and take a quick shower, not wanting him to come back and find me in another state of undress.

Because if he did, I'm not sure I could stop myself from throwing myself at him.

That would be beyond embarrassing.

I wish I had time to take care of the ache between my legs, but I know the clock is ticking. Stepping out of the shower, I dry off and put on a T-shirt and pair of jeans, hoping I look decent.

As I glance in the mirror one last time, a knock on the door sounds.

"Lia, are you almost done?" Maxim calls through the door.

"I am."

At least I hope I am.

Stepping out of the room, I give Maxim a warm smile.

"Did you get some sleep last night?"

He chuckles as he walks down the hall next to me. "I did. How are you feeling today?"

"I'm fine."

"Not fine. Whenever a woman says fine, she's never fine."

I snort. "Fair assessment. Really, I'm okay. I was a little shaken up last night, but I feel better this morning. I mean, I'm safe, right?"

"Of course. Nikolai has plans in place. I think he plans to discuss it over breakfast."

"Oh," I tell him, stopping outside the dining room.

"Let's go in. No reason to be nervous," he teases, reading me like a damn open book.

I nod, walking into the dining room in front of him. I let out my breath when I see Ivanna sitting at the table on her own. Taking the seat next to her, I smile at her.

"Good morning. How was the rest of your night?" I joke.

She scoffs. "That asshole barged back in and informed me he will be sleeping in my room until Nik tells him otherwise. I have some words for my brother. This breakfast is going to get uncomfortable fast."

I swallow hard. "Nikolai demanded to sleep in my room too."

Her eyes widen. "He did?"

I bite my lip, nodding. "He said it was for my protection. I'm assuming that's why Dimitri was in your room, too. Do you know what's going on?"

She shakes her head. "Dimitri just said he was staying in my room on Nik's orders, then took the couch and went to sleep. He didn't tell me anything. Did Nik tell you anything?"

"Only that they found something."

She goes to speak again but stops when Dimitri and Nikolai step into the room from the kitchen.

"Oh good. I don't have to hunt you down," he taunts me.

"Don't think I came because you ordered me to. I was hungry," I sass back.

His jaw clenches, but he takes his seat at the head of the table, thankfully next to Ivanna. Dimitri takes the seat across from her.

"Isn't Maxim going to join us?" I ask, glancing over at the guard by the door.

Nikolai narrows his eyes at me, but I ignore him.

"Come eat. I need my guard to be healthy and not pass out from lack of food," I say to Maxim.

He goes to argue, but Nikolai cuts in, "Of course. Maxim, join us. This involved you too."

After he does, Nikolai motions us to fill our plates. The men wait while Ivanna and I fill up ours first before filling their own. Once everyone is settled, we all start to eat.

After a few moments, Nikolai speaks. "We had a serious security breach last night. At the present, you are only to trust the people in this room. No one else. Dimitri and Maxim will be at your side at all times."

I slowly set down my fork, losing my appetite.

"So I'm not going back to school tomorrow?" I ask in a quiet voice.

He lets out a breath. "I don't want you to, but I think it's better to let everyone believe we didn't find anything. I want them to think we think you saw a guard and freaked out as some sort of reaction to the trauma of being shot. We want to catch whoever it was, which means you need to continue on like normal. So you will go to school, but both Dimitri and Maxim will be with you."

I smile. "Okay. I can live with that."

"I'm not done, Lia. That means that they check rooms before you go into them, even the bathroom." Nik looks away from me. "Dimitri told me you switched your schedule to match Lia's, correct Ivanna?"

My eyes widen as I look at her. "What?"

She ignores me. "I did. I knew when she came back, she would need an added layer of protection. This way Dimitri will be with both of us."

"Maxim will be as well. I'm not pulling him off of her just because Dimitri is there. They will each have their own priorities."

"Wait. Back up. You switched your schedule to protect me?" I grip her arm.

She looks at me with a small smile. "Of course. I got your back, girl. I wasn't going to let you come back and deal with shit on your own. This way, we can spend more time together. We will have the same homework so we can help each other. Also, we now have two bodyguards. I figured Nik would be more willing to let you come back this way too."

"That is so sweet, but you didn't have to."

"Of course I did. You're my best friend."

I pull her in for a hug, ignoring the pain in my shoulder. She hugs me back, making my heart warm.

"Are you done having your love fest?" Nikolai drawls as if he is bored.

I pull back, shooting him a glare. "Proceed, your highness."

I see the corner of his lips tilt up, but he straightens it back out quickly.

"Great. We need you to act normal, but not take any unnecessary risks. Shopping here and there is fine, but needs to be planned out ahead of time. No random trips to the park or to get food. You'll eat on campus for now as well. If you don't like the food, then pack a lunch. I'm going to need your cooperation to keep you safe."

I feel like he is aiming that more toward me than his sister, so I speak up, "I'll cooperate as long as you continue to communicate with me. I don't want to be left in the dark. If there is a threat, I'd rather know upfront so I can be prepared. I also want a knife like the one Ivanna gave me. I want a way to protect myself."

"Anything else, princess," Nikolai says sarcastically.

"Yes, actually. I don't want to be locked in a room again. I'm not going to be a prisoner, even if it is for my own safety. That's no way to live. Take it or leave it."

"What are you going to do if I say no?" he asks, raising a brow.

"I'll leave. I've made it this long without ending up dead. I think I can manage it a while longer. If not, then it was my time to go. Why stress about the inevitable? Death is going to come one way or another. I refuse to stop living my life for fear it might come sooner than I want."

A brief flash of surprise passes through his eyes, but he hides it quickly. "I can agree to those terms. Lia, I want you to think of this as home for the foreseeable future. I'm going to have you added to the safe room biometrics and I want to run a couple of simulations to make sure you understand how to use it. I won't go into the details, but shit is going down in the Bratva. Until we can be sure it's solved, I want you to be on guard."

"Understood," I tell him.

He glances at Ivanna. "That's how you should respond when I tell you what to do."

"Don't I always follow your rules?" she snarks, making me bite my lip.

He flicks a glance at me again. "I would have said yes prior to your friend sneaking into my bedroom. You risked the security of this compound."

"Lia wasn't here to harm us though," she argues.

"You didn't know that for sure, but let's take Lia out of it. You knew there was a gap in our security. You should have brought it to our attention right away. What if one of our enemies had found it?"

Ivanna hesitates. "I see your point. It won't happen again."

"Good. Now finish your breakfast."

The rest of the meal is quiet as we all eat. I'm lost in my thoughts when Ivanna speaks up.

"Can we go out to the practice range today?"

I glance over at her.

Nikolai seems to consider her question.

"That wouldn't be a bad idea. I need Dimitri today, but Maxim can take you over for a little while. No guns though."

Ivanna pouts a little at his restriction.

"What's the practice range?"

"Oh you'll find out." She gives me a mischievous smile.

NIK

"Why the fuck haven't we gotten anywhere yet?" I growl at Dimitri.

He runs his hands through his hair, showing he's as frustrated as I am.

Between the two of us, we interviewed all fifty men who were on site last night, but none of them seem suspicious. Someone is, though. One of them is working against us.

"Has Alexei found anything?"

Dimitri shakes his head. "He's gone quiet. You know how he works. He won't check in for another couple of hours unless he finds something of use. Less likely to get detected this way."

I slam my hand down on the desk. "This is unacceptable. I can't even trust my own men in my house."

"Breathe, brother," Dimitri tells me. "We will catch the rat bastard."

"I'm about to go feral. Start torturing men until someone squeals," I threaten.

He shakes his head. "You do that and you will lose all the respect you've earned. I know this is not ideal, but stay the course."

I nod my head. I know he's right. If I fly off the handle now, they will fear me like my father. While a little fear is healthy, I want their respect.

Last night, after dusting the picture and knife for prints, I had Dimitri put the items back where they were found. Unless the man was watching us, he won't know we found it. We've also placed a camera pointed at that tree to see who comes for it. So far, no luck.

We need to get a lead soon or else I might lose it. If it was only my own life on the line, I would say fuck it and practically prance out offering myself to catch the culprit.

It's not just me, though.

Ivanna. Felicity. They are potential targets as well.

I'm not willing to take a chance with their lives.

"We could always set a trap. Maybe use Felicity as bait. See if that gets a response," Dimitri says, reading my mind.

"No. Absolutely not. We will not put her in danger like that," I say adamantly.

Dimitri's eyes narrow. "You like the girl, don't you?"

I shake my head. "It's not that. She took a bullet for me. She has earned my protection."

"If that's what you want to believe, but I saw you before she was shot. You pulled her into your side as soon as Oleg started salivating over her. That was a possessive move to show him she was not on the menu. Even before that, you acted like you couldn't stand her, but I know you bought her wardrobe yourself. I even know all about your request for her bag from evidence. It's okay to like the girl, Nik."

"I…" I trail off, shaking my head. "It's not important. What's important right now is getting this hit off of us so that I can send her away like we planned."

He scoffs. "As if you will ever actually let her leave."

"I'm seven years older than her, Dimitri. She's basically a child."

"She's not a child. She is a woman. An adult woman who hasn't been a child since her mother died when she was nine. Besides, when has age ever mattered in our world?"

He has a point, but this isn't an arranged marriage. Felicity isn't part of our world. She didn't grow up in it. She doesn't know the danger she would face by staying. The demands it would make of her.

I can't entertain the idea of even subjecting her to that, even if I desire her. Besides, who's to say that after I sample her, I'd continue to want her.

No. It's better to let this infatuation run its course. Find the rat. Exterminate my enemy. Then send Felicity on her way.

"It doesn't matter. My decision is final. Focus on finding the rat and protecting my sister."

"If that's your command."

"It is."

He dips his head. "I'll head out then. Maybe you should head out to the range and offer that added layer of protection since I'm otherwise occupied."

I glare at him. I know what he is doing.

"They are fine."

He shrugs. "If anything happens to Ivanna, I will hold you personally responsible."

Standing, I move into his space. He doesn't cower or move back. He stands his ground.

"Last I checked, I'm the boss around here. I make the orders. Ivanna is my sister. Her care is my concern."

He spits right back. "You entrusted me with her care for the past three years. She may be your sister, but she is *my* responsibility. I care for her in the way that *I* best see is fit. So I will repeat myself. If something happens to her while she is outside of this house on a field trip you approved while sending me away on an errand, I will come at you for retribution."

I stare him down a moment. Any other boss would have already shot him dead for his words. Not me. This is why I chose him as my second. Why I entrusted him to care for my sister.

I laugh, clapping him on the shoulder.

"Ivanna's with Maxim. She will be fine. Hell, she isn't even leaving the property. Good to know you took my order to make my sister your number one priority to heart."

He's still stiff, but steps back. "Of course. I take all your orders seriously."

"That's why you're my second. Now get out of here. I will check on the girls in a bit to ease your mind."

He shoots a glare my way, but leaves the room. I wait until he leaves before walking back toward my desk, pulling up the cameras.

The practice range is on the back edge of the property and backs up to a lake. Father built it as an arena to test his men in all ways of combat, often putting his best against each other to fight to the death.

I stopped that when I took over. Now we use it as a training ground for the men to practice without fear of death. Not only them, but I've allowed Ivanna to train as well. She wanted to be able to protect herself and I felt no need to say no like my father did.

So when Ivanna said she wanted to take Lia there today, I didn't say no. It's not the most secure section of the property with the lake being open, but it's safe enough. Besides, I'm curious as to what Lia knows about self-defense.

Watching the cameras, I smile when I see Lia and Ivanna facing off. They each hold a knife in their hand. I watch them circle each other until Ivanna strikes out. Lia jumps back before making her own move. They keep trading jabs until Lia drops her knife, holding her arm.

I straighten in my seat. Not being able to see what's happening through the grainy screen has my heart pumping. When Maxim makes his way onto the screen, I jump up.

Before I know what I'm doing, I'm jumping in my car, driving down the narrow lane toward the practice range. When I arrive, I hop out, leaving my car running.

When I make it to the sparring area they were using, I find Lia and Ivanna sparring again.

Walking up to Maxim's side, I hiss at him, "What happened?"

He looks down at me confused. "What do you mean?"

"She was hurt a couple minutes ago."

His eyes widen. "You were watching?"

"It doesn't matter. What happened?" I snap.

"When she moved, she had a bit of pain in her shoulder. She waited a minute then went back to it."

"You should've made her stop," I grumble, stepping away from him. "Enough," I demand as I approach them.

They both stop immediately, Lia spinning to face me.

I step closer to her, grabbing her arm. Then I pull down her shirt, making her gasp.

"What are you doing?" She tries to pull back, but I hold her still.

I look over her shoulder, noting that the wound is still as it was before. Logically, I knew she wasn't bleeding, but I had to see it with my own eyes.

I press around the wound a little to make sure the skin feels okay.

She hisses in pain. "Stop. Why are you hurting me?"

I stand up straight, letting her shirt fall back into place.

"I was checking to make sure you didn't fuck up your wound. You need to be more careful."

"How did you even know I was hurt?" She shoots a glare at Maxim.

He doesn't react. He knows better than to admit anything. If I want her to believe he called me out here, he will take her anger.

"It doesn't matter. Your form is shit. You're swinging your arm around too much. It's sloppy."

"I'm new at this. All the fighting I've done was spontaneous. I've never trained," she huffs at me.

"I can see that. You're scrappy, which will help you in a surprise situation, but in hand-to-hand combat, you need strategy. You need to learn to read your opponent. For example, Ivanna here always leads with her right foot. If you watch the way her feet move, you can anticipate her next strike."

"Hey! Why are you giving away my secrets?" Ivanna calls out.

I look over at her. "If I can read you, then others can too. You need to work on your body cues. Right now, you are predictable. You need to work on that."

"Are you offering your superior training skills, big brother?" Ivanna taunts.

I step back from Lia, stripping off my coat jacket. "Why not? I want you to live, after all. Hold this for me, *kroshka*. You can have winner." I toss my jacket at her before rolling up the sleeves of my shirt past my elbows.

I don't miss the way Lia's eyes are drawn to my forearms. I can practically see her drooling. It shouldn't please me, but it does.

Once I'm done, I turn to face off against Ivanna.

"I'm going to take you down," Ivanna boasts, but we both know I can end this in a second if I wanted to.

"Show me what you got, Ivy," I tease her like I used to when we would spar as kids.

She grins as she faces off against me. She makes a couple of jerky movements meant to trip me up, but I see her intention in the way she moves her body.

"You're tensing before each move. I can tell you won't mean to come at me. It needs to be a smooth transition. You're jerking too much," I tell her, letting her continue.

After a moment, her moves become more fluid. A little harder to read, but still not impossible.

When she finally makes her move, I watch as her foot plants in front of the other as she moves toward me, her knife in her hand swinging at me. I sidestep her easily, tapping her shoulder to show I could've attacked.

"First blood to me. What next, little sis?"

She growls, spinning to attack me. This time, she doesn't give me a second to read her, but I'm still too fast. The knife runs across my upper arm, cutting away the fabric of my shirt.

"All right. Now we are playing. You can do better than that."

I let her lead one more attack, this time barely missing my side before I go on the offense.

Within three moves, I have her on the ground, her knife against her throat. "Concede," I demand.

She glares at me but admits defeat. "You win."

Standing up, I offer her a hand, but she refuses it and stands on her own.

"Don't be salty, Ivy. You still got a hit on me. I think we have let too much time pass between training sessions. We need to make it a regular thing again."

"Well, we would if you weren't so busy." She pouts.

My eyes soften a little at her words. "I'll make time for you."

She nods. "Okay. I'd like that. Lia can train with us, too. She needs more help than I do."

"Thanks for the vote of confidence," Lia says behind me.

Turning to look at her, I hold out my hand for my jacket. She walks closer, passing it to me. When my skin brushes hers, I feel warmth that I've never felt before.

"It's your turn. Prove her wrong," I say, tossing my jacket over to Maxim. I open my arms to show her I'm ready.

She narrows her eyes but takes up a position in front of me. Unlike Ivanna, Lia is not taking a fighter's stance. She doesn't stand with her arms up in front of her, knife ready to lash out.

Instead, her arms are lax at her sides, the knife held in her hand, but the stance she has taken makes her seem like she is not a threat.

I tilt my head to the side to consider her, but before I can do anything, she lashes out. The knife glints in the sun as it comes across my chest.

Instead of the pain I expect, I only feel a hard object draw across my skin.

Not taking a second to look down, I jump forward, catching her momentum to pull her to me. Before I can secure my hold, her head comes back, almost knocking me in the nose. It's enough to put me off balance.

When her legs give out, I tighten my hold around her chest to hold her up. Immediately I realize my mistake. As soon as I take on her weight, she pulls her legs back to lock behind my knees. It takes all my strength to keep upright.

Not only that, but the more pressure I put on her chest, the more I realize her breasts are against my arm. Instead of focusing on her moves, I'm focusing on what I want to do to her.

Pressing my lips to her ear, I whisper, "I think I like you pressed against my body, restrained to the point you can't move."

She takes my distraction as the moment she needs to disarm me. She drops her legs to push off the ground before flinging all of her weight forward, pulling me to the ground with her.

I attempt to keep my body from falling on hers, but the way we were positioned doesn't allow it.

"Lia, are you…" Before I can finish, she elbows me in the ribs, making me roll with a grunt.

The next second, she is sitting on me, straddling my hips with her knife at my neck.

"Concede." Her voice mimics my demand from before.

I hesitate a moment.

I can hear Ivanna next to Maxim. "Fuck, that was hot. Did you see her go all femme fatale?"

Growling, I grip Lia by the hips, flipping her to her back. Settling between her legs, I press against her.

"Never hesitate. That hesitation gave me the upper hand," I whisper in her ear, my cheek brushing hers.

I can feel her heart beating through her chest into mine. Her breaths are coming quicker.

I'm about to pull back when I swear I feel her thighs tighten around me, bringing my aching cock closer to her center. It brushes against her once, making her gasp in my ear.

Fuck, I think to myself. *This is a terrible idea. What are you doing here? Abort mission.*

Pulling back quickly, I help her stand before facing Ivanna again.

"I think you two should spar a bit more. I have some work to get done, but you only have an hour, then I want you back at the house. Dimitri is concerned about your safety out here without his supervision."

"Of course he is. He's a tyrant. Why can't Maxim be my guard? He's much nicer."

Maxim flinches at her words. Being described as nice isn't what a Bratva man would pride themselves on. No, they would rather be seen as hard. Uncaring. Ruthless.

"That's why Dimitri is perfect for you. You can't manipulate him into shit. It's why I chose him. That, and he puts your safety over everything else."

"Oh really? So where is he?" she taunts.

"Ivanna, enough. Do you want to go back to the house now?"

She crosses her arms. "No. I want to train with Lia."

"Okay then. So train and be back in an hour."

Glancing over at Lia, I address her directly. "You fight well. You can use some more techniques, but coming off as unassuming then pouncing is an excellent technique. Don't let them know you are a threat until you need to be a threat. That's a good strategy. We will start training after school every day. If I can't come down, Maxim or Dimitri will train you."

She looks surprised. "Thank you."

Nodding, I walk toward Maxim. "Keep an eye on them."

He hands me my jacket as I make my way back toward my car. The door is still wide open, the engine still running. Shaking my head, I climb inside.

I need to get out of here.

CHAPTER TEN

Lia

"Today's word is desire. Take the last twenty minutes in class and free write for me. You can take the story wherever you want as long as you have *desire* in it. Make me want what you want. You could desire to own a big house on the hill and how your want for that fuels you. Or you could write about how you desire someone. It's up to you, and by the end of the class, I want you to drop the story on the corner of my desk. Don't worry about spelling or anything of that nature, you won't be graded on that. Now get to work," the teacher says.

Half the students groan and the other half giggle as they whisper to one another.

Picking up my pencil, I think about what I could possibly write about. Desire is hard for a girl like me to think about. I rather keep my expectations low so that way when things don't happen, I'm not completely crushed.

Putting pen to paper, I think about how I desire to be strong. How I don't want to have to depend on anyone but myself. I write about how sparring makes me feel strong and confident. My pen flies over the page as I write it all down, emotion pouring out of me.

Before I know it, my brain shifts gears, and I can't help but think about when I got to spar with Nikolai. I had no idea what I was doing, but that didn't stop him from going at me. He didn't take it easy on me and I loved it.

The way his eyes flared when I took him down. Or when he flipped me over, settled on top of me, and whispered in my ear. I loved being caged in by his big body and the feel of him over me with my legs wrapped around him. I thought I had been turned on before, but Nikolai proved me wrong.

He makes me want things that are dangerous for a girl like me.

"Pst…"

"What?" I ask Ivanna, refusing to make eye contact.

You were just thinking of her brother.

"What are you writing about? You're blushing!" she whispers.

"Nothing important," I mumble as I read over what I wrote.

Miraculously, I didn't write anything about Nikolai and kept it PG. Glancing up at the clock, I see I only have five minutes left of class, so I wrap up my thoughts on paper. I make sure I have my name up in the corner and rip the paper out of my notebook. Dropping the notebook and pencil into my bag, I zip it closed.

The class starts murmuring again as everyone waits for the bell to ring.

"Are we sparring when we get back to your place?" I ask Ivanna quietly.

"Most likely." She shrugs. "You know Dimitri. He will take every chance he can to remind me who's in charge."

"Guy's got to take the frustration out on you somehow," I tease.

She rolls her eyes. "Please, I don't frustrate him. I'm a fucking saint."

"Sure…" I drawl as the bell rings.

Ivanna and I grab our bags as we stand, sliding them onto our shoulders as we step out of the classroom. Dimitri and Maxim fall into line with us. One in front and one behind as they lead us out of the school.

"Do you girls have any homework?" Dimitri asks over his shoulder.

"Shouldn't you already know that answer?" Ivanna asks.

"Nothing that can't wait. Think we can spar first when we get back?" I ask.

"I was going to recommend we do it first, anyway. There is a storm rolling in that I would like to beat."

"What, don't want to roll around with me soaking wet?" Ivanna quips.

"Are they always like this?" I ask over my shoulder to Maxim.

"Always," he says as we step outside, making our way to the car.

Dimitri and Ivanna bicker back and forth the entire way back to the compound.

Once we get back to the house, I jump out of the car before Maxim has a chance to put it in park and run upstairs to change.

"Excited much?" Ivanna smirks as she slips into her room as I exit mine.

Ignoring her, I walk down the stairs and gather my hair, putting it into a ponytail. Looking over the railing, I see Nikolai standing, talking to Dimitri. I can't help but admire the way his shirt fits across his wide back.

Nikolai looks over his shoulder like he can feel me staring at him. By the time I hit the landing, he disappears out of sight and I can't help but feel a little sad that he's avoiding me.

He's not avoiding you, he's just busy.

"Get stretched out. I'm going to change and then we will head down to the training area together," Dimitri says, pulling me out of my thoughts.

"Okay." I nod as I drop down to the floor and begin to stretch. Closing my eyes, I take a deep breath and feel my muscles stretch and pull. It hurts but in a good way. By the time I'm done, Ivanna and Dimitri are both making their way into the living room.

"Ready?" Dimitri asks.

"Let's do this," I say as I stand.

💀

Even with Maxim following me around, I still manage to slip under the radar. After finishing working out with Ivanna and Dimitri, I head to my room.

"He really isn't like his father. He's a good boss," someone says, making me pause.

I creep closer to the door and listen.

"I would gladly follow him into battle," someone else says.

"I overheard him talking to Mikhail, asking how his mother is doing. Mikhail was honest and admitted they were struggling. Nikolai gave him some extra money and offered to make a couple calls to try and get the doctors to do their jobs."

"His father would have never done that," another says in disbelief.

"Tell me about it." The men chuckle, bringing a smile to my face.

"He gave me off the entire day last week when I asked if I could leave early to attend my daughter's dance recital as long as I brought a picture of her the next day."

"And did you bring the picture, Gleb?"

"I did. Showed him a picture of all of us next to the stage with Anya in her outfit."

"He had us deliver food to David and his wife when their baby was in the hospital."

It's good to know his men are loyal.

"It is not polite to eavesdrop, Lia," Maxim chastises in my ear.

"Oh please, it's not like I overheard anything important," I whisper-shout as I push off the wall.

Silently, we walk back to my room.

"He wouldn't like knowing you overheard that," Maxim says as I reach for the handle.

I turn around and lean against the door, crossing my arms. "And what's wrong with knowing that his men are loyal to him? That he's a good boss?"

Maxim scratches his jaw, thinking. "His father was harsh and led with an iron fist. Nik wants to be nothing like him, yet he knows at times he will have to be. When those times happen, they overshadow all the good he is done. He doesn't see it the way you and I do."

"If only we could see ourselves how those around us see us," I muse.

"You two would be good for each other, you know."

"I don't know what you're talking about," I say, looking away.

"My only job right now is to follow you and keep you safe. Don't you think I've seen the way you look at him when no one else is watching? Or the way his eyes seek you out in a room?"

"It doesn't matter." I shake my head. "It's not like that."

"But it could be." He pauses. "Just make sure that this is the life you want before you go down the road. Once you say yes, there will be no turning back."

"What are you, my own fairy godfather, offering me advice?" I tease.

"Get inside. You smell." He smirks, letting me off the hook.

"Later, Maxim." I smile as I push off the door and let myself inside.

NIK

Walking into the kitchen, I come to a stop when I see Lia standing in front of the fridge, ass pointing straight at me.

What would she do if I walked up behind her, grabbed her by the hips, and pulled her into me?

Lia whimpers, pulling me out of my thoughts.

"You okay?" I ask as I walk toward her.

Lia whips around, her hand on her chest. "Jesus, don't scare me like that!"

"Sorry, didn't mean to," I say, raising my hands.

"I should put a bell on you," she mumbles under her breath.

"Where is Ivanna?"

"She needed something for school and convinced Dimitri to take her to get it and get dinner."

"Have you eaten?"

Lia shuts the fridge door and sighs. "No, but I need to."

"What sounds good?"

Lia bites her lip. "Honestly, I don't know. But I need to eat something. These cramps are killing me."

My eyes follow her hand and watch as she rubs her lower stomach.

Clearing my throat, I move toward the fridge and open it.

"How do you feel about salmon?"

"As far as I know, I've never had it."

"You up for trying it?" I ask as I grab the fish and other ingredients out of the fridge.

"Hey, if you are cooking, I won't turn it down. Food is food," she says as she takes a seat at the counter, curling up into a ball in the chair.

After turning on the oven, I grab a pan and the spices I want.

"Who taught you how to cook?" Lia asks as she watches me.

"I don't know how to cook much, but what I do know, I've taught myself. Following a recipe is easy. Find one with enough stars and you should be all right."

"Sounds easy enough, I guess."

"Tell me, how is school?"

Lia goes on to tell me about her day as I place the salmon in the oven and make a salad full of leafy greens. Once the timer goes off, I pull the fish out of the oven. Letting it rest, I make each of us a salad before placing the salmon on top.

I set one bowl in front of Lia and another next to her before walking around the island and taking a seat next to her.

"Dig in."

"This smells so good."

I watch as she takes a bite and feel my cock stiffen as she moans with her lips wrapped around the fork.

"Is it good?" I rasp.

"This is fucking delicious," she says as she goes in for another bite.

Clearing my throat, I move my fork, taking a bite. The flavors pop on my tongue and I smile.

"What made you decide to make this?" she asks between bites.

"When Ivanna first started getting her cycles, they caused her a lot of pain. I don't like seeing those I love hurting, so I looked up different ways to try and eliminate the cramps. Omega threes and leafy greens are supposed to help." I shrug.

"That's…" she trails off. "Sweet."

"Did you get your schoolwork done?" I ask, avoiding her compliment.

"I did."

"What do you plan on doing the rest of the evening?" I ask as I finish my food.

NIKOLAI

"I was thinking about watching a movie," she says as she hops down from her chair, grabbing both of our bowls. "Would you like to join me?"

"That depends," I say as I watch her rinse the bowls before placing them in the dishwasher.

"On?"

"What you want to watch. If it's anything too sappy, I will have to put my foot down."

Lia leans back against the counter and crosses her arms, smirking at me. "Can't tarnish your reputation as a hardass now, can we?" she teases.

"Never."

"Well it's a good thing I like action movies then, huh? I was thinking a little *Fast & Furious*. How does that sound?"

"That works for me." I nod as I stand. "Go get ready, I'll meet you up there in a few minutes."

I watch as she walks out of the kitchen and can't help but groan.

What are you doing? You shouldn't be spending any more time with her than necessary.

Standing, I walk around the island and begin making some tea. Then I move back to the fridge, pulling out a bunch of fruit. I wash them all before placing them in a bowl. Next, I grab two bars of dark chocolate from the pantry. I reach for the tray and place everything on it.

Grabbing the tray, I leave the kitchen and head toward the movie room. Stopping at the threshold, I see Lia lying down on her side, blanket thrown over her. She has a small smile on her face as she holds the remote in her hand.

Fuck it. I'll spend one night with her and just be.

"What do you have there?" she asks, breaking me out of my thoughts.

"Some snacks in case you get hungry," I tell her as I walk into the room, setting the tray on the table. "Here, take this," I say as I hand her a cup of tea.

"What is this?"

"It's chamomile tea with some honey."

I watch as she brings the cup up to her mouth. Her eyes flutter closed with a small smile playing on her face.

"This smells wonderful." She takes a sip. "Tastes great too. Thank you."

"You're welcome," I say a little gruffer than I intended.

"Sit," she says, patting the spot next to her on the couch.

Grabbing my own cup of tea, I sit down next to her and settle in.

As the movie plays, I can't help but pay more attention to Lia and every time she moves.

"Would you like to lie down?" I ask as she curls further into herself, trying to make herself as small as possible.

"Kind of, but I'm okay." She shrugs.

I grab her arm, pulling her closer to me. "Lie down," I say as I place a pillow on my lap.

Hesitantly, Lia lies down on her left side, with her head in my lap. Without thinking, I remove the hair tie from her hair and begin playing with it.

"That feels amazing." She hums, making my cock stir.

"Shh," I chastise. "Watch your movie."

Lia relaxes as the movie goes on and before it's over, she's fast asleep in my lap.

Looking down at her, I can't help but wish that it could always be this simple. That there could be more nights like this with her. But I know that's not in the cards for a man like me.

Shaking away the longing, I slowly slip out from under her. Reaching down, I pick her up, cradling her in my arms.

"Wha..." she mumbles, startling awake.

"Shh. Go back to sleep," I whisper as I carry her to bed.

Once in her room, with one hand, I pull her covers back and lay her down softly. Carefully I cover her up, tucking her in.

She looks so small. So innocent.

Leaning forward, I kiss her forehead.

"Sweet dreams, *kroshka*," I whisper before forcing myself to take the couch for the night.

Lying on my side, I stare at her in the dark

Tonight has been too intimate. I need to distance myself.

NIKOLAI

If I don't, then I'll give in to the temptation to take her. As much as I want her, I don't want to risk her.

CHAPTER ELEVEN

Lia

"I'm so tired of being stuck here all the time. I want to go get some ice cream or something without being tailed all the time," I tell Ivanna at lunch.

Maxim is by the door while Dimitri sits a table over, keeping an eye on the rest of the students. I couldn't believe how quickly they accepted the new additions to the school. I mean, I guess Dimitri has always been here, but more in the background. Now they are much more visible.

"What do you mean?" Ivanna asks.

"I appreciate that you and your brother took me in, but I miss feeling normal. Now, all I feel like is there is a huge target on my back. Yet, nothing has even happened. I just want a normal afternoon."

I don't mention the fact that being cooped up in the house with them has been causing some confusing feelings to rise up inside me. Especially when it comes to Nikolai. Last week, we had a pleasant night together having dinner and watching a movie.

Then the next morning, I felt nothing but coolness from him. Yet still he haunts my dreams. He thinks I haven't noticed that he has started coming to bed after me and leaving before I woke up. I know it's because he started sleeping on the couch. Still, I can't bring myself to confront him.

I need some damn space. One day where my thoughts aren't plagued by the Bratva and Nikolai.

Ivanna bites her lip. "Okay. I can make that happen, but they are going to kill us."

"Wait, what?"

"I can get us out of school without being detected. We can go get some ice cream, but there is an eighty percent chance we will get caught."

"I don't want you to get into trouble. I'm only venting. I didn't mean it."

She leans in closer. "Honestly, I've always wanted to rebel, but I was scared to do it on my own. I've never been allowed to go anywhere by myself. It would be kind of nice to go for ice cream, just us girls."

"Are you seriously using me as an excuse to rebel against your brother?"

She shakes her head. "Not him. Dimitri. Before Nik took over, I didn't have a guard like Dimitri. I mean, I still was never alone, but I was mostly ignored. Then my dad died, and Nik took over. Next thing I knew, Dimitri was my shadow. He's way stricter than Nik ever was."

"You think it's because he wants you?" I whisper to her, glancing over at the man in question.

She sighs. "If you had asked me that two years ago, I would have told you that if he did, I would ride that train, but now? I hate him. He acts like he's my parent, but he's not. I can't wait until I can get rid of him."

"So you really want to sneak away?"

She shrugs. "It will be a good test run for college because trust me, I plan to go to parties."

"Will Nikolai kill me?" I worry, biting my bottom lip.

She gives me a small smile. "No. I won't let him. Besides, if he wanted you dead, you would already be dead. He wouldn't have bought you all those clothes or got your necklace back."

My hand flies to my neck. "What? I thought you got me clothes and

Maxim gave me my stuff."

She rolls her eyes. "So naïve. Nik wouldn't let me buy you clothes. I heard he picked them out himself. As for your necklace? Only Nik could get Detective Sanders to hand over evidence."

My heart races. "Maybe we shouldn't make him mad."

"Don't go soft on me now. Do it for me. I promise he won't punish you. I'll tell them I made you and you went with me to protect me."

I hesitate. "Only because you have also been so good to me."

"Great. This is going to be awesome."

She stands, walking over to Dimitri. She whispers in his ear. His eyes meet mine. I look down, not wanting to give away that I'm nervous. After a moment, Ivanna comes back.

"Let's get you to the bathroom."

Dimitri follows us to the first girl's bathroom we find.

After he clears it, he gestures us in.

"Maxim is getting you a change of clothes," he tells me.

I give him a small smile, not knowing what he is talking about.

"Great. Let us know when he gets here. Thanks for being delicate about this," Ivanna tells him, popping up to press a chaste kiss to his cheek.

He gives her a weird look, but nods.

After the door closes, she moves to the window, sliding it open.

"Perfect. I was hoping it wouldn't be locked. Now help me up, but be quiet."

Following her lead, I hoist her up so she can climb out the window. Once she is seated on the ledge, she helps pull me up.

It only takes us three minutes to get out of the bathroom.

"Turn your phone off, otherwise they can track us."

I nod, watching as she does the same.

Then we take off running.

It only takes ten minutes to get to the ice cream shop. Once inside, the weight on my chest lightens a bit.

"You think they are looking for us?" I whisper to Ivanna.

"Oh, I would bet they are."

The whole run over here, we kept quiet. Both too tense to break the silence.

"What did you tell him to get him to leave us alone in the bathroom?"

She chuckles. "I told him we had a code red situation, and that you were not prepared. When he asked what I meant, I told him you were bleeding like Niagara Falls from your vagina and desperately needed a change of clothes and ultra tampons. He wanted to pull us from school, but I explained that I truly meant a waterfall and that you were embarrassed and worried you would bleed through your clothes. I told him you wanted to sit on the toilet until they could bring you something to wear. He got all weird after that."

I burst out laughing. "Jesus, I hope I never need a tampon in public. They will never help me again."

She's laughing with me. "Of course they will. They just might make you go with them. Especially when they realize a vagina stopper is not a real item."

"You didn't." I laugh.

"Oh I did."

We had seen a social media trend where women tell their male partners or family members to buy them a female hygiene product, but it's made up. The results were hilarious, especially if they dared ask the store associate.

"They are going to kill us," I groan out.

"Ice cream is worth it. So what will it be? My treat." She pulls a twenty out of her bra.

I shake my head. "Good, because I don't have any money."

Once we get our order, we sit and eat it, talking about everything from cute boys at school to what we want to do for the future. It's a lovely afternoon. For once, I feel like a normal teenage girl again.

As time flies, the sun starts to set.

"Maybe we should head back," I tell her, my nerves getting the best of me again.

"Probably a good idea. Here, I'll turn on my phone and order us an Uber."

After several minutes, we're on our way back to the compound. Once at the gates, I know we are in trouble. The guard glares at us as he lets the driver take us to the front door. Walking up the steps, I consider running. For once, I think I regret a decision I made.

NIKOLAI

As soon as we make it through the door, I know I'm in trouble. Not only me, but Ivanna too.

"Where the hell have you been? Don't you know the danger you're in?" Dimitri bellows at her.

Nikolai comes into the room a moment later, his eyes meeting mine.

"Lia, come with me." His voice is eerily calm.

"No," I tell him, planting my hands on my hips.

He shakes his head. "It wasn't a request. Come with me or I will pick you up and carry you."

Ivanna reaches down to grab my hand. "It's okay. Dimitri and I need to have a talk about how to speak to a woman, anyway. I will come find you soon."

Nodding, I walk to Nikolai, following when he turns to lead me into the study.

Spinning, he glares at me. "You promised cooperation. Leaving the house without permission or a fucking guard is not cooperating."

"You know, it's been two weeks and not a single person has tried to hurt us. No security breaches. Nothing. Why are we still on lockdown?"

"Haven't you ever heard that there is quiet before the storm? They could be waiting for us to become complacent. To take advantage as soon as we let our guards down. What if someone had snatched you up? How did you even get home?"

"Uber. Believe it or not, I have survived worse before you."

"You don't make those decisions anymore. I have half a mind to lock your ass up until I no longer want to strangle you for being so careless."

"You don't own me, Nikolai. I am still a human being. I have rights."

His chuckle is dark. "You don't even know about the world, *kroshka*. There is no such thing as true freedom. It is all an illusion the government maintains to keep the cattle in check."

"Well, either way, you definitely don't own me. I don't have to obey your stupid rules."

"As long as you live in my house, you will abide by my rules."

I scoff. "I have been trying to leave for weeks. You refuse to let me under the guise that it's not safe for me. Tell me, is that even true? Am I truly in danger?"

"You are in more danger than you even realize. I will tell you one more time because I'm feeling generous. Follow the rules set forth or face the consequences."

I roll my eyes. "What's the worst you can do to me? Lock me in my room?" I snark, gasping as his hand shoots out, grabbing me.

He pulls me into him as he makes his way to the chair by the fireplace.

Before I can question it, he sits, lying me across his lap.

"What the fuck are you doing?" I attempt to get off his lap.

His arm comes down between my shoulders while his other hand flips the end of my skirt up. I feel the cool air against my thong-clad ass, making me shiver.

"Nikolai, let me up."

He lets out a humorless laugh as he lightly touches me. "You asked about consequences, now you are going to face them."

Without warning, his hand lands on my right ass cheek with a resounding *whack*.

I squeak, my body jolting as it stings. The sting turns into a throb, making my center ache. I take a deep breath, my cheeks heating with the warmth spreading through my body.

When the second hit comes to my other ass cheek, my breath catches. My nipples pebble beneath my bra as my body reacts to this punishment as if it was a reward. Breathing hard, I bury my face into his leg. I can feel how wet I'm becoming with each new smack. Once he is up to five on each cheek, he rubs the area, making my body tremble.

I can feel the evidence of my arousal leak down between my legs. I attempt to squeeze my legs together, not willing to let him see what he has done to me.

"Do you understand now?" His voice is husky as his hand continues to rub my ass.

"Mmhmm," I hum, trying to hold back the moan from the way he is making me feel.

I must not do a good job. Next thing I know, his hand slips down until one finger presses between my legs.

"*Fuck,*" he curses beneath his breath. "Did you like your punishment?"

I open my mouth to deny it but nothing comes out, so I shake my head no.

"Such a pretty liar."

Then he slips his finger beneath the material of my thong straight to my hot core. He swipes his finger over my clit twice, sending sparks flying through my system. Then he moves down, sliding one inside me.

Unable to help myself, I arch into his hand. I know I should stop this. Nikolai only wants control over me. He doesn't want me as anything more than a toy. I should be repulsed by this, but I'm not.

A part of me wants to be his toy. To experience everything he has to give, even if it means he will throw me away later.

That's the only reason I can think of to explain why I'm lying still on his lap while he slowly fingers me.

I can feel his erection under my stomach telling me he likes this as much as I do.

He leans down, pressing kisses to my lower back as his fingers pick up the pace. I can feel the pleasure building higher and higher. Promising an explosive climax. My body takes over as it moves with his, chasing the fall.

"Lia, where are you?" Ivanna calls out from a distance.

Jolting, I whimper, trying to move away, but Nikolai doesn't let up. If anything, he moves faster, his thumb moving to stroke my clit hard.

"Better come quick if you don't want to get caught," he rasps quietly.

I gasp, realizing what he means. He won't stop even if she walks in.

"Nikolai, please," I beg.

"Hush now. Take the pleasure while I'm feeling generous. Feel how good it can be when you obey me."

His words are like crack to an addict. My body sings for him as he continues to whisper what a good girl I am and praising my body.

Within seconds, I am right on the edge.

"Come all over my fingers, Lia."

His command washes over me, my body contracting around his fingers, attempting to milk them for something only his dick can give me.

After several moments, he finally slows before stopping completely. Once he pulls his fingers out, he flips me over, pulling me close to his chest.

"Next time you disobey, I will bring you to the edge all fucking night long until you go crazy with need with no relief."

I swallow hard, nodding an understanding.

He presses a quick kiss to my forehead, letting me go.

"Run off now. Ivanna is looking for you."

On shaky legs, I make my way to the door, listening to Ivanna call me from down the hall. Before I step out, I look back, catching Nikolai sticking his fingers in his mouth, sucking them clean. The same fingers he had inside me.

My body shivers at the erotic scene, my center heating back up, begging for more. Before I can give in, I run out of there, almost crashing into Ivanna.

"Where have you been?"

"Sorry, I was talking to Nikolai," I tell her, pulling her away from the study.

"Everything good? You are all flushed." She frowns.

"I'm fine. I just stood too close to the fireplace."

"How mad was Nik?"

"Well, he didn't pull a gun on me this time, so I don't think he was that mad," I joke as we walk up the stairs.

"That's not funny," Ivanna huffs as she stomps up the stairs.

"Hey, you have to admit that it's a little funny now that we can look back on it."

"If you say so."

"Do you think we missed anything important in any of our classes today?"

"Nice subject change," Ivanna says, raising a brow as she turns at the top of the stairs. "Probably not. To be safe though, I will text a couple people to find out to cover all of our bases. God forbid we fall behind." She rolls her eyes as she steps into her room.

"I hate being behind." I cringe as I sit down on her couch.

Leaning back, I shut my eyes as Ivanna talks about who knows what. I can't help but shift on the couch thinking about the way Nik had his hands on me. He made my body sing in a way that I've never accomplished on my own and it makes me a little jealous.

I need a cold shower.

"Are you even listening to me?"

"Sorry, I zoned out. What were you saying?" I say, making Ivanna sigh.

NIK

Walking down the hall toward my study, I pause when I hear her.

"What in the actual fuck."

Stepping forward, I lean on the doorframe and watch her. Lia's hair is up in a messy bun with pieces framing her face. She's curled up in the chair with a book in her lap.

"Are you going to keep creeping or are you going to join me?"

"That depends," I say as I push off the doorframe, walking toward her.

"On..." she says, turning and giving me her full attention.

"Would you like company?" I ask as I sit.

"You can do whatever you want, it's your house." She smirks.

Shaking my head, I look around the library. "It's nice seeing someone take advantage of this room. I don't remember the last time I came in here."

"It's one of my favorite rooms in this place."

"Then I'm glad you found it," I say, watching her blush. "What are you working on?"

"Do you really want to know?" She tilts her head.

"I wouldn't ask if I didn't," I say as I lean back, making myself comfortable.

"My history teacher is offering up extra credit. All I have to do is find the most ridiculous thing that has happened in history and write a short paper on it."

"So you came to the library."

"So I came to the library." She smirks. "And let's just say I've found some truly ridiculous things that have happened."

"Like..."

Lia leans forward with a small smile on her face. "Did you know one time in eighteen sixty-five during a navy battle between Brazil and Uruguay, the Uruguayans ran out of ammunition so they used cheese instead..." She pauses. "Cheese, Nikolai. Fucking cheese."

I laugh. "Did it work?"

"It worked enough that the Brazilians retreated," she says, shaking her head, laughing with me.

"What else have you found?"

"During the Battle of Frigidus, the Western Roman army lost because of a windstorm. Which led to the Eastern Roman army to bring Christianization to Europe."

"Seriously?" I say in disbelief.

"Look it up," she challenges.

"All right," I say, raising my hands. "I'll believe you. Have you come across the Battle of Pelusium?"

"No, tell me."

"Picture this, a war has been brewing between Egypt and Persia and finally things come to a head. You're an Egyptian and you see the Persians advancing on you…" I pause dramatically. "With cats strapped to their shields."

"No…" she says breathlessly.

"Oh yes. And you can't do anything because it's illegal to kill cats. Since you can't kill them, the enemy overtakes the city, winning."

"I can't even…" She shakes her head. "Did anyone die?"

"I don't know the numbers, but I remember that the Egyptians lost a lot and the Persians very few."

"I think I know what I'm writing my paper on now." She laughs, shutting the book. "Fucking cats."

"Well, I guess I better let you get to it," I say as I lean forward, about to get up.

"Or…"

"Or?"

Lia bites her lip, shrugging. "You could stay."

"I could." I nod.

"Just don't distract me, okay?"

"I wouldn't dream of it," I say, fighting a smile.

Pulling my phone out, I send a quick text to Dimitri telling him where I am. Then I check my emails.

Sitting here with Lia is oddly comforting. You would think it would be awkward to sit in a room with someone and not speak a word to each other, but being in her presence is enough.

This is why I was keeping my distance. I knew I was losing myself to this spell she has weaved around me. Anytime I'm in a room with her, I gravitate toward her.

Almost like I need to be near her.

It's what brought me in here today. Hearing her voice, I couldn't help but take a peek at her.

I never expected her to ask me to stay.

Yet I did.

Fuck. This is a terrible idea. I need to get out of here.

I go to stand, making her eyes snap up to me.

"You're leaving?"

The look of disappointment is almost too much. I almost sit back down.

I don't though, I hold strong.

"As much as I enjoy your company, I have work to do. Let me know if you need any more help with your paper."

She gives me a small smile. "Oh. Alright then. Thank you for spending a little time with me."

I turn to leave, but then walk over to her at the last minute, pressing a kiss to the top of her head.

"I can stay a little while longer if you'd like."

"I don't want to keep you. I'll be okay if you need to work."

I can hear Dimitri in my head.

This girl has you by the balls.

I can't even deny it anymore.

I can act like I'm going to let her leave eventually, but it's too late for that.

The girl is mine.

Now I just need to tame her.

"I'll stay a little longer."

CHAPTER TWELVE

Lia

I grab the tablet Ivanna gave me off the side table and pull up the Battle of Pelusium. Nikolai walks toward the bookcase and runs his fingers along the spines. Taking a deep breath, I shake my head and switch the tablet over to split screen and start taking notes.

Why did he stay?

My mind wants to overanalyze the whole situation. He was leaving, which I didn't like, but understood. Then he looked at me and changed his mind.

I have no idea what is going on with us, but there is this chemistry that is undeniable.

I don't want to ignore it anymore.

I attempt to focus back on my paper. Every so often, I can't help but look up at Nikolai.

"Tell me, *kroshka*, do you even need the extra credit?" he asks with his back turned toward me.

"No, but extra credit is always nice to have. Why do you ask?"

"Because if you keep looking at me, you won't get anything done. Now hurry up and do your work, I won't be the cause of you falling behind."

"Who says you are distracting me?"

Nikolai looks over his shoulder, eyebrow raised. "I can feel your eyes on me. Work."

"Yes, sir," I sass, making him freeze.

Smiling to myself, I get back to work. Before I know it I have enough notes to write the short paper and begin. The paper basically writes itself. I save the document and turn off the tablet, setting it back on the table. Looking over, I see Nikolai sitting in front of me, holding a book.

Who knew a man reading could be so attractive?

"Did you finish?" he asks without looking, with a smile on his face.

"I did."

"Tell me, why do you use a tablet instead of a laptop?" he asks while shutting the book, resting it on his knee.

"It's easier." I shrug. "I like the size and how easy it is to carry. Besides, that's what Ivanna gave me and it's better than what I used to have to do."

"And what did you do before?"

"I had to write everything out by hand and then go to school early to type it up and print it off of one of the school computers."

Nikolai makes a face before schooling his features. "Would you like a laptop?"

"No, I'm good with what I have." I pause. "But thank you for asking."

"Why wouldn't I ask?"

"Let's be honest, Nikolai. You're more of a do something first, ask for forgiveness later."

"Nothing wrong with that." He smirks.

"What were you reading?" I ask, looking at the book on his leg.

"Nothing important. Tell me, *kroshka*, if you could go anywhere, where would you go?"

"I honestly don't know," I say thoughtfully as I think about all the pictures of places I've seen. "I want to go everywhere and see everything." I shrug. "Really I just want to live. To experience as many things as I can. Try different food, meet new people. What about you?"

"Traveling for me has never been an option outside of going back to Russia. Would I like to? Yes. But I'm not the type to wish for things that I know will not come true."

"That's kind of sad." I frown.

"How so?"

"Wishing goes hand in hand with dreaming and everyone should have some sort of dream. Long term, short term, it doesn't matter. Dreaming is good for you. It makes me sad that you don't dream for something because you'll never know what it feels like when those dreams come true."

"Have you ever had a dream come true?"

"Yeah, I dreamed of when I would finally escape the system. Granted, it wasn't pretty by any means, but the relief is undeniable."

Nikolai tilts his head to the side and stares at me.

"What?" I ask, shifting in my chair.

"How about I let you dream enough for the both of us?" he says, making me speechless. "Now, I saw some cards in a drawer over there." He points to the other side of the room. "Would you like to play a hand or two or would you prefer to go to bed?"

"I-if you're willing to teach me how to play I'm game."

"Good."

I watch as he stands, moving to get the cards and I can't help but think about how he is so much more than I ever could have imagined.

He's lethal but caring. He acts like he doesn't pay attention but he asks the right questions. He can pull random history facts out of a hat and gives you his complete attention when you speak.

He makes me want things that I don't think he's willing to give.

"Are you ready?" he asks as he sits down, breaking me out of my thoughts. "Should we get snacks or anything to drink before we start?"

"Sure."

I watch as he pulls out his phone and types out a message before setting it to the side.

"I messaged Maxim to bring us a few things. Now the rules are simple," he says as he launches into the rules of the game.

Part of me wants to tell him I already know them from when I played with Maxim, but I can't bring myself to do it. I enjoy hearing his voice.

His hand brushes against mine as he deals the cards, and I can't help but shiver.

Nikolai raises a brow and smirks. "You good?"

"I'm fine," I say as I shiver again. "Please continue."

Nikolai shakes his head but does as I say, making me smile.

He is patient as I attempt to play the game. We laugh and snack as we play.

"Shit," he says as he looks at his phone.

"What's wrong?" I ask quietly.

"It's almost midnight and we both need to get to bed."

"The leader of the Bratva needs his beauty sleep?" I tease as I stand, stretching my arms above my head.

"It's for your own good. Good girls like you need to be tucked away before the bad things can come out to play," he rasps as he devours me with his eyes.

"Good girls are just bad girls who haven't been caught."

Nikolai stands, stepping toward me. He brings his hand up, cupping my chin. "And men like me love corrupting. I'll see you in the morning. Sweet dreams, *kroshka*," he says before stepping away and out of the room.

Taking a deep breath, I follow him out and make my way to my room. Once I reach the door, I rest my hand on the handle and look over at him one last time.

"Don't let the bedbugs bite," I say quietly before stepping inside.

I head straight for the attached bathroom and flip on the light. Stripping off my clothes, I toss them into the hamper and get a look at myself in the mirror. My breasts are full, nipples pebbled. Turning, I stare at my side profile and can't help but arch my back, thinking about the way it felt when Nikolai touched me. The ache builds between my thighs and I can't help but rub them together.

All night the slight touches while we played, the heated looks and teasing put me on edge. He stroked a fire he didn't even know he lit.

I walk into the shower and turn it on as warm as I can. Leaning against the wall, I stare into the mirror and run my hands from my collarbone down to my nipples and tweak them, making myself gasp. Trailing one hand lower, I lightly touch myself, running my fingers over my lips as I tweak my nipple. I gasp as I start to massage my clit. Rubbing a little harder, I pinch my nipple and bite my lip to hold in the sound.

I continue to play with myself, trying to get myself there, but it's not enough.

I need Nikolai.

I have never felt this needy before.

Groaning, I give up and turn the shower to cold. I shiver as the ice cold water hits my nipples as I wash my body. Quickly, I get out of the shower and get ready for bed. Once I lie down, the need to come has lessened, but it's still there.

I wonder if I could sneak a toy in here and how Nikolai would react if he found it.

Or better yet, what would he do with it? I think as I fall asleep.

NIK

THE GIRL IS trouble. I only planned to stay a little while with her in the library, but I spent the entire evening there. We didn't even leave for dinner.

I hate that I found the way she pouted when she lost a hand adorable. I hated even more how badly I wanted to pull her into my arms and kiss her until she couldn't breathe.

This loss of control I feel inside is new. I have never had to deny myself the impulses it wants. Even in business, I am rarely impulsive.

Yet with Lia, that's all I am. Every time I enter a room with her in it, I have to resist the urge to go to her.

She's across the hall getting ready for bed and all I want to do is go over there and crawl into bed with her. To slide my body against hers, feeling her skin pebble with my touch. Run my nose along her neck into her hair and smell the fresh scent of jasmine that clings to her.

My dick throbs in my pants. I've been hard all night. Being so close to Lia, yet denying my need to touch her, has been torture. I was hoping it would be like immersion therapy, but I'm nowhere near getting over her.

The more exposure I have to her, the more my body aches for her.

It's not just her body, though. If it was, I would fuck her and get it over with.

No, I like her mind as well. She is witty, intelligent, and has a damn backbone that both infuriates yet entices me.

She is the total package.

She deserves better, but I know it's too late to send her away. Whatever this is, it needs to run its course.

I scroll through my messages and reports from the foot soldiers until I'm certain that Lia is sound asleep. Then I slip inside her room.

Sitting on the edge of her bed, I look down at her. She really is beautiful.

For a moment, I considered making Maxim sleep in here with her, but the burning rage at the thought changed my mind real quick.

I guess that should have been the first red flag that this girl was a problem.

Yet, I let her stay. I can't imagine letting her go now.

I stroke her hair before leaning down to press a kiss on her forehead.

She grumbles in her sleep a moment before settling again.

I glance over at the couch. It's where I've been sleeping. A boundary I put in place for myself to help resist the temptation.

Yet tonight, I find myself curling up next to her, my arm wrapped around her center. She immediately turns toward me, seeking my heat.

"It's okay, *kroshka*. I'll protect you," I vow to her.

Pressing another kiss to her hair, I settle in.

I will do whatever I can to make sure whatever happens, that she will be okay. I won't let any more bad touch her.

CHAPTER THIRTEEN

NIK

I was tempted to peek in on the training session today, but I was able to resist. Just barely. If it wasn't for the interruption from the guards at the gate, I might have given in.

"Oleg is here, sir," the guard calls through the phone.

I tense. He never comes to the house.

"Escort him through to my office."

Hanging up the phone, I dial Dimitri. "Maxim is to stay on the girls and keep them away from the house. I need you here now. Oleg is here."

"On my way."

He hangs up without further comment. A few minutes later, I hear the knock on my door.

"Come in," I call out, not bothering to get up.

Oleg will see this as a slight, which is what I mean it to be. I'm the boss. I only stand if I feel you are owed respect and I'm not sure Oleg is owed that. Especially since he showed up here unannounced.

"Have a seat," I tell him.

"How are you doing?" he asks as he sits.

I entertain his small talk, buying time for Dimitri to get here.

"Fine. What about you, Uncle?"

"Quite all right. Life is grand, isn't it?"

I stare at him without expression.

He slaps the arms of the chair. "Well, I am here for a reason. What happened to the girl you brought to the restaurant? Did she perish?"

I grit my teeth, trying not to show emotion. I don't like the look in his eye. "She didn't, thankfully. Especially since that bullet was meant for me."

"Ah. What did you do with her?"

"How is that any of your business?" I ask, raising a brow.

"Is the girl becoming a problem, nephew? Seems she has crawled under your skin."

I bristle on the inside at his accusation but attempt to keep my cool.

"Not at all. She has value, though. Value I'm not quite ready to give away."

He chuckles. "Is she tight?"

I force a laugh to my lips. "She's not my type."

"Whatever you say. I still think we should trade her to Jakub. She would fetch a pretty penny at market. Especially if she's still intact like that foster father of hers claimed."

I try not to let his insinuation sink into my head.

"Oh? I didn't know that trading her was an option. You talked to him?" I act disinterested, but I'm really fucking interested as to why my uncle has been talking to a nobody would-be rapist.

"He's one of Jakub's guys. Uses that foster home to filter girls through the system. If they go missing, oops." He shrugs. "Another foster kid ran away. The state doesn't give a shit."

I barely bite back my seething response. I could kill my uncle right now, but that would be impulsive. I've learned in my life that being impulsive leads to mistakes.

Not only is he saying they are running girls, but that man's home is in my territory. Or at least it was until he disappeared.

"Well, she's mine for now. My decision is final," I instill my authority behind it.

Oleg bows his head in submission. "Of course, boss."

I don't like the bite to his tone, but I ignore it for now. I have bigger problems. Like what I am going to do about the blatant disrespect from the Polish.

Still, there is that nagging part of my mind reminding me of the last time I was in a room with my uncle. Something is going on here.

"If that is all, I have other things to do."

"Of course. Thank you for meeting with me."

I watch as he leaves. As soon as he's gone, Dimitri steps in.

"What was that about? You look ready to murder someone."

"He no longer has open access to this home. I want to know every time he shows up here."

"Understood. I'll relay the message."

He pulls out his phone, but I stop him. "Verbal. I don't know who he has loyal to him. He didn't fight me for this position after my father's death, but that doesn't mean that he doesn't have his own men within our ranks. I've let it go this far because our agendas aligned, but that is not the case anymore."

"Got it. Do you want to talk about it?"

"He wants to sell Felicity at the meat market."

Shock and confusion cover Dimitri's face. "Seriously? We got out of that after your father."

"I know. Seems uncle dearest still dabbles in it with the Polish. I won't let him have her."

"Of course not. If you really want to protect her, you know what you could do."

I wince at his insinuation.

"She will hate me."

He smirks. "Do you really care? I thought we were protecting her because of what she means to your sister."

That's what I said. I meant it when I said it too, but my uncle was right. Somewhere between the late-night meals and quiet time in the library together, she has become important to me too.

"I promised her she could leave when it is safe."

"She caught your uncle's eye. She will never be safe again. Not until he stops breathing. So unless you plan to kill him, this is our next best option."

I run my hands over my face. "Fuck. I know. You're right. Let me talk to her first."

"And if she says no?"

I hesitate. "Then I'll make the decision for her."

He nods. "When do you want to do it? The sooner the better."

"Tomorrow evening. I'll talk to her at dinner. Keep Maxim on her for now. She trusts him. I need you to keep Ivanna occupied tomorrow. Find something that will distract her, then come down at nine. If she says yes, I won't need you, but if she says no, I'll need you to keep her still."

"Understood. For what it's worth, I think you're doing the right thing."

I sigh, rubbing a hand over my face. "Let's hope she agrees."

Lia

"So, what's going on with you and Nik?"

My eyes widen at Ivanna's question. "What do you mean?"

She shrugs with a small smile on her face. "A little birdie told me he wants to have dinner alone with you tonight. Sounds like a date. Are you dating my brother?"

Her voice is teasing, but my heart still races.

"No. Of course not. He's your brother. Girl code and all. Besides, he's like nine years older than me and a powerful Bratva boss. What would he want with me?"

I can feel my face blushing at the thought that he would want me at all.

"He's only seven years older than you. He's twenty-five. You're fucking hot as hell. Not to mention you are smart, too. Of course he wants you. As for girl code, I give you my permission, but maybe just don't give me the dirty deets. That would be weird." She cringes.

I shake my head. "He didn't even ask me to dinner tonight. Until you brought it up, I assumed we all would be having dinner together again."

"I'm telling you what Dimitri said. He told me we would be dining in my room and watching a movie and that at one point he will need to run a security check, but that we were on our own. When I asked him why, he said Nik wanted to have dinner with you alone."

My heart hammers in my chest. That little bit of hope swells up.

Does he feel what I do?

Does he want to touch me again as much as I want him to?

I remember the way his hand brushed mine in the library. The way my skin pebbled as my body heated from the fleeting touch. I thought I was imagining it.

A harmless crush on my friend's older, hot brother. A rite of passage for every girl.

Maybe my feelings aren't quite unrequited.

"I can see you thinking a million miles a minute. Live in the moment for once. You aren't in a foster home. You're eighteen and safe for once in your life, and a man you think is hot wants to have dinner with you. Let's doll you up so you can enjoy your night."

Pushing my homework away, I groan, "I never said he was hot."

"You didn't have to. I see the way your eyes follow him when he's in the room. You can't hide the blush on your cheeks every time he speaks to you. Trust me, you think he's hot."

I huff out a breath. "What if I get all dressed up, and he only wants to have dinner to tell me it's all safe now and I can leave? That would be so embarrassing."

She shakes her head. "He wouldn't. Besides, if that was the case, he wouldn't be sitting down to a meal with you. I know my brother. Trust me."

I sigh. "Fine, but you need to help me."

An hour and a half later, I'm showered, dressed, and ready to go.

I step in front of the mirror, gasping at what I see. I have never spent much time on my appearance. I didn't want to draw the wrong kind of attention.

Looking at my reflection now, I don't even recognize myself. I mean sure, my hair color is the same. My facial features haven't changed, but talk about a glow-up.

I look sexy.

The blood red dress Ivanna picked out is perfect. It ties behind my neck, leaving a deep V between my breasts. My entire back is bare, landing right above my ass. There is for sure no room for underwear in this dress.

"Wow," I breathe out.

"You look like a bombshell. My brother is going to drool when he sees you." Ivanna claps, looking giddy.

"You really think so?" I question, letting my nerves show.

"I do. It's almost eight. Go get him, tiger." She winks at me.

"Wish me luck," I say under my breath.

"You don't need luck."

Heading out into the hall, I take a deep breath. I can't believe I'm going to do this. For once in my life, I feel my age and inexperience.

I walk toward Dimitri in the hall, chuckling when he does a double-take.

"Well, Lia. You clean up nice. You look beautiful."

I blush, smiling up at him. "You don't think it's too much?"

He shakes his head. "It's perfect. He's waiting for you in the dining room."

That makes me feel better. If he doesn't think I overdressed, then maybe Ivanna was right.

"Thank you."

He gives me another reassuring smile before heading toward Ivanna's room. I continue down the hall, stopping outside the dining room.

Taking one last deep breath, I step inside. I immediately gasp at what's before me.

The table is set for two. Candles lit around with a pretty bouquet decorating the table. Standing next to the chair at the head of the table is Nikolai. He is dressed impeccably as usual, but something about tonight makes it feel special. Like he went an extra step to look nice.

For me.

Like I did for him.

I feel his eyes on my skin as he takes me in.

"Lia, you look absolutely stunning," he says as he takes a step closer.

I swallow hard, my skin heating at his attention.

"Thank you," I squeak out.

He smirks as if he knows what he is doing to me. Cocky bastard, but I can't fault him for it. He is sex on a stick and he knows it.

He leans in, pressing a soft kiss to my cheek before whispering in my ear, "Come. Let's eat."

I give him a small smile when he pulls back. When I take a step toward my chair, his hand falls to my lower back, making my skin tingle.

He pulls out my chair, helping me sit. Then he uncovers a serving platter. The aromatic smells from the pot roast flood my senses.

"This is my favorite," I say wistfully.

"I know. Ivanna told me," he says as he sits down.

My heart warms. Why did he ask Ivanna what I would like? I think back to the way he has made me feel.

Is he feeling this too?

As he fills my plate, I take a moment to really study him.

He is handsome. I have never had issues admitting that. He has this rough and rugged look to him. Like he has survived many fights and has the scars to prove it.

Still, even with the rugged look, the suit he wears fits him perfectly. It adds a layer of refinement. I can see tattoos peeking out from his wrists and at his neck, but he covers them well.

The facade of a proprietor hiding the tales of a true king.

"Would you like some wine?" Nikolai asks, bringing me out of my musings.

"No, thank you," I tell him.

He smirks at me. "If you're worried about age, I promise I won't tell."

I smile back at him. "I've never been one to really drink. I don't like the way it makes me feel out of control."

His eyes flash, an understanding settling on his face.

"Tell me about your past," he says. It comes out as a demand, but I can see the intention in his eyes.

I intrigue him. He wants to know more about me.

Part of me worries when he finds out who I really am, he won't have a need to keep me around anymore. I mean, I'm a boring nobody. I have no ties to his world, nor do I understand it.

Still, the other part likes that he wants to know me. Like he might be under the same spell I've found myself under since the night I climbed through his balcony.

"My childhood was great. My parents were wonderful. Well, I don't remember much of my father. I was only five when he passed away, but I remember missing him. Mom used to always show me pictures of him and tell me about him. Mom did her very best to always care for me. Even when she struggled, she made sure I never felt like I missed out on life."

"How did you end up in the system?" he asks gently.

I shrug. "My father passed away from cancer when I was five. I barely remember it, but I do remember wondering why more people didn't come. Mom said his family had disowned him because he ran off and married my mom so young. I guess I was an unplanned pregnancy and when his family found out, they wanted her to abort me. He took what money he could and ran off. Mom never had any family. She was a foster kid like me. They met in high school. When he got sick, she was going to school to become a nurse, but she ended up dropping out, settling for a certified nursing assistant. After he died, Mom picked up more hours at work. She'd take even the worst hours if it meant a little more money. When I was nine, she was on her way into the graveyard shift when she was hit by a drunk driver. I was told she died instantly."

My eyes tear up at the memory. She was all I had.

Nikolai reaches out, grabbing my hand in his.

"I'm so sorry for your loss."

I nod, sniffling. "Anyway, when she worked nights, she left me alone and locked the doors since I was sleeping. I woke up to the police at the door. Once they realized I was alone, they took me in. They did this whole family finding thing to try to place me with a family member, but Dad's family wanted nothing to do with me. They never found anyone on Mom's side. So into the system I went."

Nikolai clears his throat. "That's a rough hand you were dealt. You've done an amazing job to get to where you are today. You're strong and brave." He leans forward, brushing a piece of hair from my face. "Beautiful."

My heart ticks up its pace. Unable to accept a compliment, I fall back on my default. Humor.

"I've sure handled it well. I ended up getting into countless fights to protect myself, only to the end up taking a bullet for a Russian boss and become his prisoner," I tease, shooting him a smile, letting him know I'm only kidding.

His eyes grow dark. "You're not a prisoner here, *kroshka*."

I shake my head. "So I can leave right now? Walk out the front door?"

I already know the answer before he voices it.

"No, but for your safety. You're not our prisoner. You are a guest that we wish to protect."

This time, I turn my hand over, squeezing Nikolai's. "It's okay, Nikolai. I understand and appreciate your protection. Sometimes I feel a little caged, but as long as I remember the reason for the cage, I feel better about it."

"It won't always be this way. I'm doing everything I can to eliminate the threat so you can go on living your life in whatever capacity you wish."

I pull back, nodding. "I know that. It's why I am still here and not fighting."

I take a bite of my food, unable to take his eyes on me anymore. It sounds like he is only keeping me until he can be sure I won't die because of my actions to save him.

"Well, you did sneak out before. Are you saying I don't have to worry about you trying that again?"

I quirk an eyebrow at him. "Technically, we snuck out of the school. I'm not saying that was our best idea, but the intention was pure. You should really let us go out more. Staying inside these walls makes both Ivanna and I go a little crazy."

He sighs, setting his fork down. "I know that. Maybe I can loosen the reins a little. What would you do for a bit of freedom?"

My breath catches as I consider his words.

Is he flirting with me?

"I, um, what did you have in mind?" I ask him, looking down at my plate.

He chuckles. "Your cheeks heat so easily, but I can't say I mind the view. The red on your cheeks is almost as appealing as the red on your ass after I spank it raw."

I. Stop. Breathing.

One second I'm in the room with Nikolai enjoying dinner.

The next, I'm back in the study, bent over his lap as he smacks my ass. The feel of his fingers gliding through my center. The sparks I felt through my system as he brought me to a place I have only ever felt when he touched me.

I'm brought back from my thoughts when a soft touch caresses my face.

"You know I had to go back to my room after that display. Here I thought I was punishing you, yet you ended up enjoying every second of it," he says gruffly.

My eyes open at his words, his face so close to mine.

"Tell me, how often have you thought about it? Have you reached between your legs and stroked yourself to thoughts of what I did to you?"

I sway closer to him. "I tried, but it didn't feel the same."

A smile spreads across his face. "That's right, *kroshka*. Only I can make you feel that way. Do you want me to make you come now?"

I feel a hand on my thigh, lightly tracing.

"I…" I trail off, unsure how to answer.

My body wants to. Oh, does it want to give him everything but my emotions? They are all over the place. All those questions swirling in my mind.

What does this mean?

Are we going to have sex?

Should I tell him I'm a virgin?

What if I disappoint him?

Will I be able to face him after this?

"It's okay, Lia. Take your time. Think about it. I'll expect an answer by dessert."

He moves back to his seat to eat his dinner.

I stare at mine, unable to form a coherent thought. Something about his dominant personality calls to me. Almost as much as it frustrates me that I want to adhere to his commands.

After a few moments of silence, I clear my throat, desperate to move on to more neutral topics.

"Tell me about Russia, you said before that's the only traveling you've done, right?"

I don't meet his eyes. I know if I do, I will end up throwing myself at him, which would only embarrass me more.

"Yes. When I was younger, my father thought it was prudent to show me where we come from. That was before my mother was murdered. After that, he focused on his business here."

My eyes fly to his. I had no idea his mother had been murdered.

He gives me a sad smile. "She was murdered when I was thirteen. Ivanna must have been six. It was tough on Ivanna. All she had was Mother. My father did not value women in this business. So he hired a nanny to watch over her, but after a couple months, I realized she was mistreating Ivanna. I demanded my father fire her and he did, but then Ivanna became my responsibility. On top of the shit I had to do for him, I had to care for her. That meant finding protection when I had to be away."

"Is that why Dimitri is on her? He seems pretty important to you."

Nikolai chuckles. "Observant. Dimitri is my second in command. Back then, I rarely used him as a babysitter for Ivanna. I often used some of the younger recruits closer to her age. It wasn't until my father was murdered and I took over three years ago that I assigned Dimitri to her. It wasn't until then that she needed a constant presence."

"What changed?"

"My father was cruel. He would torture, mutilate, and kill anyone who got in his way. His punishments were inhumane and often ended in death, even when that was not the intention. Because of this, he was feared. No one dared lay a hand on Ivanna because she was his. He had been brokering possible marriages for her when he died. Taking over for him, I did not have that same reputation. I had to build it from scratch. That and I took Ivanna off the table for good. It put a target on her back."

"Your father was really willing to give her away to someone? Why?" I frown.

"I forget sometimes that you are so innocent. In my world, you marry off your daughter, sister, niece, or whoever you can to gain political ties. I could offer Ivanna up and make a deal in exchange for access to more territory, money, new business, or items I need. Hell, I could do it solely to secure an ally. However, I refuse to do that to my sister. In many ways, I feel like she is more like my child with the way I raised her. I don't want this life for her, but it is the one she was dealt. So I will give her the choice of man she wants to marry, but I will still have to approve. It's the only way I can ensure her happiness, and that she's protected."

I swear another chink in my flimsy armor comes down. I can tell he means every word. He went against what his father would have wanted, what many men in his position would have done because he respects his sister more than that.

"That's admirable. I'm glad you care about her that way. I'm not sure we would have ever met had you not."

"How *did* you meet my sister?"

It's my turn to chuckle. "Your sister met me. On my first day of school, some asshole jock was trying to convince me to go out with him. No matter how many times I said no and tried to move around him, he kept pushing. I was just about to say fuck it and punch him when your sister jumped in and kicked him in the balls. Dimitri obviously made his presence known when the guy's friends moved forward. Once they left, she decided we were going to be friends. Even when I tried to shake her, she stuck to me like glue."

"Is that why you told her what was going on?" he asks, tilting his head to the side.

"I mean, at first she could tell I wasn't getting enough sleep. She would ask questions, but never anything too invasive. I guess she wore me down. After a while, I was sharing with her without her asking. Next thing I knew, she had me cutting class one day to teach me how to use that knife. Dimitri wasn't pleased, but she refused to budge."

"I wonder why Dimitri never mentioned these events to me," he muses, almost as if to himself.

"I have a feeling Dimitri only tells you things he feels are important. You are a busy man, after all. Why would you care if your sister made friends with the new foster kid?"

He rubs his chin. "Good point. I probably wouldn't have cared."

My heart aches a little at the admission. He only cares because I made him care. I burst into his life and placed myself right in front of his face.

"Are you finished with your meal?" he asks the next second.

I look down and realize that I've cleared my plate sometime along the way. "Yes."

He removes the plates, reminding me again that I have never seen any servants here other than the maids that clean the home.

I know he cooked for us once before, but I wonder who normally does the cooking.

"Who cooks for you?" I ask when he walks back carrying two plates and dessert.

He laughs. "I usually cook for myself unless we are having a large number of people over or I want something specific."

"So no servants?"

He shakes his head no. "I prefer to keep my household staff at a minimum. The fewer people you invite into your home, the less chance you will be stabbed in your bed while you sleep."

"Is that why you were so surprised when I climbed through your balcony door?"

"You should have never made it that far. My men failed me. They are lucky you were you and not an assassin sent to kill me."

"I think you had a handle on it. You took me down pretty quick." I smirk.

"I hesitated. I normally wouldn't have. You are lucky to be alive, honestly. I didn't take you down. You passed out on me," he points out.

My cheeks heat again. "I had run several miles, climbed a wall, avoided your cameras and guards, then climbed your balcony. I was exhausted. I'm surprised I even made it in your room."

He reaches out, his thumb rubbing my bottom lip. "I'm glad you did."

With that, he unveils the dessert, a New York cheesecake with strawberries over top. Another favorite of mine.

"Wow. That looks delicious."

"You'll have this for dessert, then maybe I can have you for dessert."

My eyes widen, but he only smirks, setting the plate in front of me.

"Thank you," I tell him, unsure if I am going to eat even a bite with that visual on my brain.

"Dig in." His eyes are glinting with humor.

Is he fucking with me?

What does it mean that I hope he is serious?

Unable to keep up with my brain, I use my fork to break off a large bite. Once the taste hits my tongue, I let out a moan.

"This is just like I remembered. I haven't had cheesecake in years."

Opening my eyes, I find Nikolai's on me. More specifically on my mouth as I lick the excess food from my lips.

"Keep moaning like that and I'll get jealous," he rasps.

"Of cheesecake?" My tone incredulous.

"Yes. I'll have to prove that I can make you moan longer and louder."

I can't help it. I laugh at how ridiculous he is being.

"It's cheesecake. I don't think it cares if you can make me moan."

"No, but I care that it's making you moan right now when all I want to do is dive between your legs."

I almost choke on the bite I had just placed in my mouth. Without a second thought, I blurt out, "What is wrong with you?"

His eyes flash with surprise. "What do you mean?"

"You are being really forward tonight. Like coming on really strong. What's going on?"

"Maybe I'm tired of fighting against my cock every time I see you."

"You really want me?"

"*Kroshka*, I don't just want you. I need you." He reaches over to grab my hand, placing it in his lap against his very firm erection. "Feel how bad I need you? Every time I think about you, my cock ends up like this. Hard and throbbing. Aching for your touch. What are you going to do about that?"

I freeze, thinking about it. What am I going to do about it?

Pushing back my chair, I make the decision. Nikolai lets go of my hand, his eyes resigned when I stand.

He must think I'm leaving. That I'm rejecting him.

"Lia, we need to talk," he grits out.

I ignore him, falling to my knees next to his chair.

His eyes flash to mine.

"You asked me what I'm going to do. How about I show you?" I whisper.

I don't know where the sultry tone comes from, but all I know is I'm in the moment.

For once, I don't want to focus on my over-analyzing mind. I want to let my body lead me.

He scoots back his chair, angling it toward me. I slip easily between his spread legs. Reaching up, I unbutton his pants, dragging the zipper down.

I grip his erection, squeezing it softly before pulling him out of his boxers.

Fuck. I didn't realize how big he was. Who am I kidding, I have never actually seen a dick outside of naked pictures on the internet.

How the fuck am I going to fit that in my mouth?

I stroke him a couple of times, pondering my question when he speaks.

"Grip me tighter," he demands.

He grunts when I do as he asks, but his eyes remain on my hand on his dick.

After a few moments, I lean forward, licking the drop of liquid from the head.

Nikolai hisses above me, his hand reaching down to caress the side of my face.

"You are a fucking wet dream on your knees like that for me. Do you know how sexy you look right now?"

I fight the smile, attempting to cross my face. I never realized I needed praise until he started giving it to me.

Wanting to make this good for him and needing that praise, I lean forward, taking him in my mouth. Slowly, I lower myself until I gag. Then I pull back.

"Fuck, your mouth is so hot and wet."

Repeating the action, I press my tongue against him while I suck. When he groans out more dirty words, I smile around him.

I pick up the pace, using my hand to stroke what I can't fit in my mouth. After several minutes, I have a good rhythm going, only gagging every couple of passes.

I can feel his cock throbbing inside my mouth, growing even bigger, if that is even possible. When his hand tangles in my hair, his hips thrusting to meet me, I know I must be doing it right.

As I keep going, I can't help but rub my thighs together, turned on by turning him on.

Only a couple more passes and he bursts, the salty flavor of him spilling down my throat.

I force myself to swallow every bit. I wait until he stops jerking before pulling him from my mouth.

I wipe the corner of my lips, smiling to myself.

I didn't realize how powerful that would feel. Not to mention the throb I feel between my own legs. It was like I was controlling him, even when he had his hand in my hair. I made him lose control to the point where he came down my throat. That's a heady feeling.

Before I can contemplate my feelings, he pulls me up, crashing his lips to mine as he settles me in his lap.

His tongue dives into my mouth as he shows his appreciation.

Then he pushes back. Lifting me to my feet, he pushes the dishes back on the table before laying me on it.

"What are you doing?" I manage to breathe out.

He smirks at me. "I want my dessert," he says as he pulls up my dress, hissing when he notices I went without underwear.

"Such a bad girl coming down here with nothing under this pretty dress. Were you hoping I'd take a taste?"

He nips at my inner thigh, making me squeak.

"I asked you a question, *kroshka*."

"I didn't want panty lines," I deny weakly.

He smirks up at me. "Sure. I'll let you believe your lies. How about a little taste?"

Leaning in, he swipes his tongue through my folds, moaning much like I did with the cheesecake. Chills cover my body at the purely erotic sound.

"You taste even better than I remember. Do you know how many times I wanted to spread you out and eat you until I quench my desire?"

Before I can bother responding, he begins to devour me. I swear his tongue moves at a pace that my mind cannot process. When his fingers join in, teasing my hole, my brain shuts down.

I can feel my body moving, my thighs tightening around his head, my fingers in his hair, but the sensations flowing through my body make it so I can't focus on any single thing. I feel a slight burn as he adds a third finger thrusting in and out of me. When he spreads them, I swear I see stars. The slight bite of burn added with the intoxicating feeling of his tongue lapping at my clit sends me over the edge. Before I can even say his name, I'm flying, my body an ocean of euphoria.

For several minutes, I live there. In the in-between. When I finally come back to myself, I can feel Nikolai between my legs, his tongue now lazily tracing my center. When he reaches my clit again, I twitch, the feeling so good yet almost painful.

He chuckles, his eyes meeting mine.

"Welcome back."

I can feel my face burning red at his words. Of course he noticed I was blissed out for several minutes.

He stands up, leaning over me to take my lips with his. I can taste a sweet, exotic taste on his lips that I realize is me.

He tastes like me.

Somehow, that makes me even hotter.

I go to tell him I want to do more, but when he pulls back, his words freeze me in my place.

"I'm going to mark you right here."

His fingers are circling over my hip as he says the words.

"What do you mean, mark me?" I ask him, more curious than anything.

"There's a mark I can give you for protection. My initials, but it will hurt like hell. I want to give it to you. Will you let me?"

My heart beats faster. He wants to give me a mark? Something to show

I'm his and will offer me protection?

After what we just did, the night we shared, my mind comes to the conclusion that he must be feeling what I am. Why else would he want to do this for me?

"Yes," I breathe out.

He nods. "Let's go to the study. Dimitri should already have the fire going."

I'm confused by that statement, but I follow him anyway. I'm glad when he wraps his arm around me. My legs feel like Jell-O as my body processes the increased levels of oxytocin in my system. I have seen such a different side to him tonight.

By the time we make it to the study, there's no denying that I'm half in love with Nikolai.

CHAPTER FOURTEEN

NIK

I feel like a piece of shit, but I can't dwell on it. I didn't mean for things to go as far as they did at dinner.

I was only teasing her. Then she dropped to her knees, and I lost all control.

I have never wanted a woman the way I want my *kroshka*. There's something about her that makes me act like a fool.

So when I decided I was going to mark her on her hip, I didn't consider that she would ask why.

When I told her it was a mark of protection, I was telling the truth. It will protect her, but I wasn't completely honest as to why it would.

Still, as we walk through the study doors, I can't bring myself to take it back.

I will do whatever I need to in order to protect her. Even if she hates me for it later.

I mean, at the end of the day, she's going to leave one way or another. There is no way she would choose this life when she has another choice.

Would she stay if you asked?

Shaking away the thought, I keep propelling us forward until we are standing in front of the coffee table situated in front of the fire.

"Do you have it?" I ask Dimitri.

He nods, handing me the brand he had made with my initials.

I hold it in my hand, wondering if I can actually do this. When I place it in the fire, Lia gasps.

"Are you going to burn me?" her quiet voice asks.

I move back toward her, taking her face in my hands. "I don't want to, but it is necessary. This is my only way of protecting you. It will allow you some more freedom and give me peace of mind. Tell me right now you don't want it and I won't do it," I lie.

She tells me no, Dimitri will hold her down and I'll do it anyway. It will hurt more, but the decision has been made.

Her breaths are coming a bit faster, but she nods.

"I can handle it."

"I know you can," I lean in, pressing a kiss to her lips.

I can still taste her. It's driving me a bit crazy and makes me want her again. Maybe I'll have another go once we are done. We can't take it further. Not with her wound being fresh, but I can at least give her orgasms until she passes out.

I avoid the questioning look on Dimitri's face when I turn back to the fireplace. I'm sure he thought we would have an argument on our hands.

I thought we would too, but that's not how it played out. I know if I told her what it really means, she wouldn't be so willing, but I want her cooperation. I want this as painless as possible.

"Are you sure you don't want a shot of vodka or something?" I ask her.

She shakes her head. "I'll be fine."

"I brought first aid and a pain pill," Dimitri advises.

I nod my thanks to him.

"Dimitri is going to hold your hands above your head and your shoulders down. I'm going to sit on your thighs. I need you to lie across the table."

She moves herself into position, but tenses when I begin to move her dress up. Her concerned eyes meet mine.

"Dimitri, do not look at her cunt. If you do, I will place a bullet in your brain. Understood?" I say, not looking away from her. I watch as her eyes widen at my crudeness.

"Of course. I will keep my eyes on hers," he replies.

He moves into his position over her, his face locked on hers.

When I move her dress up, I smile as her skin pebbles. Then I frown when I realize what I am about to do.

I can't focus on it, though.

"This is going to hurt like a bitch," I tell her, pushing through my own discomfort.

Then I pull the branding iron from the fire. I take a second to ensure it is facing correctly, then I press it to her skin.

She cries out, her body jerking, but I move the brand away, tossing it back at the fire.

"It's okay, baby. You did great. You are so brave. So strong," I tell her, pushing Dimitri out of the way to kiss her face.

Tears fall freely, and I can't help but lick each one away.

After a moment, she quiets down, her tears still coming, but she seems out of the worst of it.

Dimitri stands next to me, holding out the first aid kit.

Once I take it from him, he helps Lia sit up a little, then hands her a pill and a bottle of water.

After she takes it, she lies back down, her eyes closed.

"You're dismissed, Dimitri. Close the door on your way out."

He nods, leaving us alone.

I go to work, applying the burn cream gently to the area. After that, I use medical tape to secure the gauze over it to keep it clean.

When done, I lean in and kiss right under it.

"I am so proud of you, *kroshka*."

"It hurts," she whispers.

I stand, moving by her head so I can take her lips with mine. After several chaste kisses, I pull back.

"I know. Thank you for letting me do this for you. I know it hurts. If I could have taken the pain for you, I would. The fact that you knew it would hurt and still did it means you are a badass."

"I don't feel so badass right now," she mutters as she sobs.

"Let me take care of you."

She nods, shaking as she cries harder.

Moving around to her other side, I pick her up in my arms. She immediately wraps her arms around me.

I carry her all the way up to my room. We have been sleeping in hers, but tonight I want her in my space. I owe her that.

Sitting her on the edge of my bed, I work at removing her dress. She lets me, not even turning red when I have her completely naked. Turning, I find a T-shirt, placing it over her body.

I was planning to worship her more, but seeing her look so broken only makes me want to hold her.

Pulling up the comforter, I gesture for her to get in. Once she does, I undress quickly before sliding in next to her. Thankfully, she's facing me, attempting to stay off the injured hip. I pull her into me, placing her head on my chest. I press a kiss to the top of her head.

After several moments of silence, I speak. "My father was a cruel man. He did many things I never approved of. I ended the human trafficking in our territory when I took over. I stopped the mail-order bride program too. I refused arranged marriages unless they came directly from the female themself. I do whatever I can to reverse the truly terrible things he did."

"You are an amazing man." Her voice is hoarse as she speaks.

"I don't believe that. I still murder people, *kroshka*. Torture them when I have to and have their blood on my hands. I'm not on the right side of the law."

"Maybe there is no right or wrong side of the law. Maybe there is doing the best you can while still attempting to make the world a better place. You stopped the human trafficking. So what if you steal, lie, and cheat the rest of the time? You saw something truly evil and stopped it."

"I wish I could see myself through your rose-colored glasses."

"You don't have to. I'll be here to remind you."

I press another kiss to the top of her head. "The reason I told you this is because I want to give you something. Part of me no one else knows."

She turns her head so she can look up at me. "You can tell me anything."

Taking a deep breath, I confess, "My father used to abuse me. He would hit me, use knives, hell, he even shot me once so I would know the pain of a bullet. He wanted to mold me into the perfect heir. Just as cruel and ruthless as he was. He got the ruthless part right, but I don't have it in me to be cruel like he was. I would much rather show mercy and end it quickly than draw it out. The only time I do is when we need information and a lot of times I step away and let one of the others handle it. Truth is, I'm weak. I can't stand the sight of blood or the screams of someone being tortured. All it reminds me of is my childhood. Reminds me of the screams of mine that were never heard."

Lia reaches up, caressing my face. "You are the strong one. You have to deal with that all the time and yet you're still standing. That's not a weakness. It shows your strength."

"Even when I walk away and leave someone else to deal with it?" I scoff, shaking my head.

"Especially then. It shows that you know your limits and can remove yourself before it becomes a problem. Being a leader doesn't mean being cold and callous. It has nothing to do with your ability to kill a man or make them speak by nefarious means. You know what the characteristics of a good leader are?"

"Tell me."

"Having the integrity to follow your own moral compass against all other's opinions and views. It's taking care of your men the way you would want to be treated, which I know you do. I see the way you offer praise when they do well or how you gave Mikhail extra money because his mother has been sick. It's the way you take the time and care to know your men, so you know they need these things. Not to mention the way you never send your men somewhere you wouldn't go yourself. I have heard many stories about you, Nikolai. Your men respect the fact that you are on the front lines with them. When you go into battle, you never send your men in alone while you sit back and watch from afar. Not one person in this world is perfect, but you are the leader they need."

My chest tightens with each word she speaks.

"Maybe I shouldn't give you freedom. How did you see all of that from your cushy prison cell?" I joke with her.

She sees my joke for what it is. An attempt to lighten the mood.

"I'm a ninja. Lock me up all you want, but I'd still find a way out."

Leaning down, I capture her lips with mine. "You are one hell of a woman, *kroshka*."

She winks. "I know."

When she yawns, I know her pill has kicked in.

"I really am sorry about all the pain you have been caused because of me," I tell her.

"I know. As long as I'm here with you, I don't care."

A pang of guilt hits me. This girl is trusting me blindly, and I've already betrayed that trust.

"Rest," I murmur against her hair.

I lie awake thinking about all the ways I have failed her, long after her breathing evens out.

Lia

"Where were you?"

Ivanna's voice startles me as I enter the dining room.

"What do you mean?"

"Nik came and got Dimitri this morning so I headed to your room to get the deets from the dinner last night, but you weren't there."

"Oh, Nikolai brought me to his room last night," I tell her absently.

I really need some coffee. My head still feels foggy after the pain pill from last night. The ache on my hip almost makes me wish I had another, but I can handle it. I feel like that's all my life has been. Nothing but pain.

Yet, this pain is different. The reasoning for it is different. While it aches, it also reminds me of what happened last night. The way Nikolai opened up to me.

I can feel the stupid smile fill my face.

"His room? Oh god, I do not want to know if you fucked my brother. Wait, did you? No, don't tell me."

I shake my head. "Relax, I still have my virgin status. Nikolai was different last night. More open. I enjoyed my night."

"He opened up, huh? If you wanted to know more about him, I could have told you a million stories. Like the time his pants split at the San Francisco Gala. That was great." She chuckles to herself.

"I don't want to know all that stuff from you. I mean, I love you, but I want to know what he wants to tell me. It means something different when it comes from him."

"Uh-oh," she mutters, making me frown.

"What?"

"You're falling in love with my brother. Like that is a terrible idea, Lia. He is going to hurt you." She grimaces.

I frown. "Who said anything about love. I'm getting to know him."

The lie tastes bitter on my lips. Of course I'm falling for him.

Stupid girl.

She shakes her head. "I can see the hearts in your eyes. Nik has never wanted to do the whole marriage and kids thing. I think it's because he basically had to raise me. I'm telling you now, girl, don't go there. I thought this was physical. If I had known you were catching feelings, I would have put my foot down last night."

My blood starts to boil. "So I'm good enough to fuck your brother, but nothing else? Glad to know what I'm worth."

I stand to leave, but she grabs my hand, hitting it off my hip.

I hiss in pain, making her freeze.

"What happened?"

Before I can stop her, she's pulling my shirt up to see the white gauze over my mark. She pulls it back slightly, frowning when she sees what it is.

"You let him do this to you? Are you fucking stupid?" she hisses, pure rage is on her face.

"He said it's for my protection. He wants to protect me. Is it really that hard to believe that he might actually want to keep me? That for once someone might not want to toss me away when they are done with me? Why else would he put his mark on my skin if not to keep me?" I snap back.

"That mark isn't a good thing, Lia. He branded you for market. Like human trafficking markets. He basically marked you as his personal slave."

I can feel the blood drain from my body.

"He did what?" My voice is quiet.

Her eyes hold sympathy now. "He didn't tell you."

"He said it was to protect me," I whisper, feeling nauseous.

"I'm going to kill him." She takes off toward his office.

I'm only steps behind her, but when we get to the office, we find it empty.

Turning to Maxim, I make my first demand of the man. "Tell me where he is."

Maxim, who must have heard our entire exchange, looks upset. "He's on a job with Dimitri. I'm to watch you both until they are done."

I shake my head, holding my hand out. "Dial his number."

He hesitates before doing as I ask.

I pull the phone to my ear, hearing it ring before he answers, "What's wrong?"

I growl, "What's wrong? How about the fact that you spouted all that shit about stopping human trafficking, yet you fucking branded me to be sold or some shit after lying and telling me it's for my protection. I fucking hate you. If I thought Maxim would let me walk out of this door, I would."

"You don't understand—" he starts, but I cut him off.

"No, you don't understand. From now on, I will sleep alone. Maxim can sleep on the couch or I can sleep in with Ivanna, but I no longer want you in my bed. I want nothing from you. Fuck you and your protection. I want out of here."

I hang up the phone, my eyes now tearing from the anger and pain.

"I'm still going to kill him."

I smile at her. "I know. Can we just eat ice cream and watch some bloody movies? That will make me feel better."

"Your wish is my command."

As we turn to leave, Maxim stops me. "Lia, I had no idea. I do not agree with his actions."

I pat his arm. "I know. I appreciate that."

Then I leave him to follow as Ivanna loads up a tray with several varieties of ice cream and spoons.

I smile at her.

I might have been wrong about Nikolai, but Ivanna really is the best friend a girl can ask for.

CHAPTER FIFTEEN

Lia

It's been a week since that fateful night with Nikolai.

I'm not sure if I'm thankful or disappointed that he hasn't tried to talk to me once.

The first night, I slept in Ivanna's room with her. I didn't want to know if he had come to my room hoping to cuddle me like he had been.

The second night, I decided to be an adult and go back to my room. I stayed awake the entire night, waiting to hear him come into my room. He never did.

Instead, Maxim slept on the couch in the corner.

Logically, I know he never cared. Why else would he brand me in such a disgusting way and lie about it? All he had to do was be straightforward from the start. Yet if I'm being honest with myself, I only agreed because I was swept up in what a romantic gesture I thought it was. I'm so fucked up.

I guess that's why I still held out hope that he cared. That it didn't mean what my brain was telling me it meant.

That's what happens when you follow your heart instead of your head. You end up waiting for a man who will never come because you are nothing more than a pawn.

So a week later, I'm sitting in my room attempting to read instead of analyzing my life.

A knock on the door interrupts me and, for once, I'm thankful for the distraction.

Going to the door, I open it to find Dimitri standing next to Maxim.

"Come with me," Dimitri says.

I narrow my eyes at him. "Where?"

His jaw tics in annoyance. He hates when Ivanna questions him, so I bet he hates when I do it too.

"It doesn't matter. Come on."

"If you won't communicate like an adult, then I'm not going to follow you. Contrary to the brand on my hip, I'm not a dog that follows commands," I say, crossing my arms over my chest.

His eyes flash with regret.

Yeah, buddy. I didn't forget that you were there, too.

I have given him the silent treatment ever since, but it hasn't been hard. He rarely speaks to me anyway.

"He's taking you to Nikolai's office," Maxim says under his breath.

Dimitri gives him a dirty look before looking back at me. "Now you know where. Can we go?"

Rolling my eyes, I wave him ahead of me. Once he turns, walking away, I fall into step behind him. I don't want to speak to Nikolai, but I know I will never escape from here until he lets me. Maxim is always with me and I don't have it in me to dupe him again to get away. Out of all of them, Maxim has been the kindest to me. I don't want to know what kind of consequences he would face if I escaped on his watch.

We walk in silence all the way to Nikolai's office. Once there, Dimitri gestures for me to go inside.

I paste on my best resting bitch face before stepping inside.

Nikolai is as attractive as I remember. I was hoping now that I knew the truth, that he would seem duller. That's not the case. If anything, he looks darker today. More dangerous and tantalizing.

Refusing to fall back into that hole, I focus on him as I stop before his desk. I refuse to speak first.

He stares at me for a long moment before he finally gestures to the seat next to me.

"Please, have a seat."

"I'd prefer not to. What do you want? Was I not clear on the phone?" I grip on to the anger festering inside me, wielding it like a weapon.

"You don't make the demands in this house. Now sit your ass down."

"As I told your lackey, I'm not a dog. I refuse to obey such demeaning commands."

Nikolai stands, slapping his hand on his desk, making me flinch at the loud noise.

"I have had it with you, Felicity. You will do as I command, or you will cease to exist. Make your choice quickly because I do not have the patience to deal with any more of your bullshit."

Did he just threaten my life?

My heart aches at the realization. I truly never meant anything to him. I let him touch me. Gave him my first orgasm and here he sits talking about ending my life as if it is trivial.

Gritting my teeth, I sit in the seat, crossing my arms over my chest.

"Glad to see you have some sort of survival instinct. You might yet make it out of this alive. Now, tonight we are going to a meeting. I'll have the dress I expect you to wear sent up. Ivanna will do your makeup and hair. This meeting is important, so you will obey my every command. If not, I will not be responsible for the consequences."

"Yes, sir. Will there be anything else? Do you need me to suck your cock? Shine your shoes?" I bite out at him.

His eyes harden before he moves around the desk to stand in front of me. He grabs my throat, squeezing so tight my air is cut off. As my eyes start to dance with black dots, my hands reach up to grip his wrist.

After a few seconds of me clawing, he lets go, making me gasp for air.

"Understand that I have been easy on you so far. That ends today. You will be obedient and keep the sass to yourself. If you follow the rules, you will make it through the night unharmed."

"And if I don't?" I ask, unable to stop myself.

"Let's just say where we are going, they enjoy punishing disobedient pets, but not in the same way I enjoy punishing you. My hands will be tied."

I roll my eyes. "Don't act like you care. You wouldn't save me either way. You put me in this position."

"No, you put yourself there when you stepped in front of that bullet."

"Yeah? I wish I hadn't. Then you'd be dead and I would already be moving on with my life."

His eyes darken. "Watch yourself, Felicity. You're walking a dangerous line. Are you sure this is the route you want to go?"

I push against him to stand. "I'm going to go get ready. I guess I have a date with a psychotic asshole who is hell-bent on making my life a living hell."

As I turn to leave, I hear him mutter, "At least you have a life to live."

I don't dignify it with a response, making my way out of the room. Dimitri is standing there with another man.

"Lia, this is Anton, he will be assigned to you along with Maxim."

"Do I really need another guard?" I ask in disbelief.

"Anton will walk you back to your room," he says, ignoring my question.

I nod, following the man. Once we are a few steps away, Anton speaks, "Are you okay, Miss Lia?"

"Yeah. Just a victim of the circumstance."

He frowns, but I paste on a smile. "I get to go out on a date with the boss man tonight. Isn't that where most women want to be? I'll be fine."

He nods. "If you are sure."

Maxim is still standing outside my door when I make it back. "Do you stand here even when I'm not here?" I tease him.

"Ivanna is inside waiting for you. She seems upset."

I nod. She must know about tonight.

I open the door to find her sitting on the edge of my bed, worry in her eyes.

"Please tell me you told him you wouldn't go," she begs.

I frown. "Of course I did, but you know your brother. He took all my choices away to the point that I'm now going, so let's not dwell on it. Help me get ready so I can get this stupid night over with."

Her eyes are sad as she approaches me. "I'm going to get you out of this. I promise."

"It's not your fault, Ivanna. I got myself into this mess and I'll get myself out of it."

She shakes her head. "You don't have to do everything alone, Lia. I'm here for you and I always will be."

"I know. I appreciate it. I really do, but Nikolai is never going to let me go. Not now. I will figure something out eventually, but for now, let's try not to make him mad."

"Okay. Well, go get into the shower then. I would shave like everything. The dress he picked out is very… provocative."

I let out a humorless laugh. "Of course it is. How long do we have until he said I needed to be done?"

"He told me to have you done by six. It's four now, so two hours."

"I'll be out in twenty then."

I take my time in the shower, not really caring about being on time. Part of me wants to rebel and not wear what he chose, but I know if I don't, he will probably make me change anyway. Is this a battle I want to pick?

Sighing, I finish up my grooming before getting out of the shower. When I step back into the room, Ivanna hustles me back into the bathroom to blow-dry my hair. An hour later, I am standing in front of the mirror looking like a different person.

I stare at my image in the mirror. I look sensual. Like someone who could steal your man without blinking.

The dress Nikolai chose isn't as skimpy as I had expected. After learning that he practically made me the equivalent of cattle to men in his line of work, I figured I would be wearing two scraps of fabric barely concealing my private bits.

Instead, the dress is more conservative. The fabric wraps around me like a puzzle, each strip forming perfectly to my body. The final product leaves sections of the dress cut out such as my hips, the sides of my breasts, and my cleavage. The hem falls to midthigh, but hugs me so tight, I'm not sure I'll be able to sit down without it riding up.

Add in the sexy waves Ivanna put in my hair along with the dark, smoky look to my eyes, and I look like a temptress.

"Wow," I mutter under my breath.

Ivanna smiles behind me.

I turn to her. "You did an amazing job."

She shrugs. "The palate was already gorgeous. I only needed to add some accents to highlight the best features."

She takes in my form one last time, frowning when she reaches my hip. I reach down, touching the brand.

That was the first thing I noticed when the dress was in place. My brand on my hip is proudly displayed like a badge of honor.

"I hate him," Ivanna says, full of disgust.

I shake my head. "Don't. That's your brother. He's your only family. Don't hate him on my behalf. I don't agree with his actions, but I know in my heart that when it comes to you, you are his number one priority."

She sniffles. "If that was the case, he would make you a priority too. I don't want anything bad to happen to you."

I walk over, unsteady in my heels. Once I reach her, I pull her into my arms.

"I'll be fine. You've been teaching me how to be a badass. I can handle this."

She smiles. "I know you can. At least let me give you some advice. I don't know where he's taking you, but if you're supposed to be like the girls my father used to bring home, they will be looking for submissive behavior. No talking back. No eye contact with the men. They prefer you look at the ground. If they touch you, you're supposed to let them. Follow Nik's lead."

I nod. "How do you know all of this?"

"I used to sneak around and listen. I know I was young, but I remember Father always bringing these girls in. They looked underfed and terrified. He would train them in the cages in the basement. I only saw them a couple of times before Nik caught me. After that, he explained Father was doing bad things and one day he would stop them. It took him some time, but he eventually came through on his promise."

"I'm glad he did, even if he seems to be going back on it now."

She shakes her head. "That's what makes me so angry. Why would he do this when he never liked it before? It makes me wonder what the bigger plan is."

"You think he has a plan?"

"Oh, Nik always has a plan. I just wish he would share it with us."

I nod. "Me too."

A sudden knock draws my eye to the door.

"Ladies? Are you ready?" Maxim calls through the door.

Looking back at Ivanna, I smile.

She smiles back wickedly. "Let's go show my brother how bad he fucked up."

NIK

Tapping my foot, I look over to Dimitri as we wait in the front hall.

"If she is not down here in two minutes, you are going to get her," I growl at him.

He nods. "Maxim said they were almost done."

I wanted to pick Lia up at her door, but I knew I couldn't. This wasn't a real date. Hell, I don't even want to take her with me, but when I received the invitation, I couldn't turn down the opportunity to show the brand off. The more people who see her as mine, the more likely the threat to her life will diminish.

I'm about to bitch again when I hear heels on the marble floor. Turning toward the stairs, my mouth falls open.

She is a fucking goddess.

The golden dress I chose only makes her look even more ethereal. The cutouts are perfectly placed to show enough skin to entice but still leave some to the imagination.

Those lips, though. She painted those perfect, pillowy lips a dark red. I feel like she's tempting me to take a bite.

When she finally reaches the bottom, I shake my head, remembering what tonight is all about. I take a couple of steps toward her, grabbing her hand to lace it into my elbow.

"You look beautiful," I whisper to her.

She snorts but doesn't make a comment otherwise.

Ivanna steps in front of us before I can lead her outside.

"Move, Ivanna."

"No. You listen to me"—she pokes her finger in the middle of my chest—"you might not care about what happens to Lia, but I do. If she comes back with even a single scratch on her, you will regret it."

I laugh, raising a brow. "What are you going to do?"

"I'll accept a contract for marriage for someone who lives on the East Coast so I never have to see your manipulative face again. I love you, brother, but Lia's safety is a hard limit for me," she says in a serious tone.

I swallow hard, glaring at my sister. She would take this girl's side over mine.

Gritting my teeth, I give her what she wants. "As long as Lia follows my rules, no harm will come to her."

Ivanna gives a curt nod. "Good."

Turning to Lia, her face softens. "You'll be okay. I'll see you when you get home."

Lia smiles at her. "I got this. Now enjoy your night. Make Dimitri watch the *Twilight* movies."

I hear Dimitri groan as Ivanna's face fills with a devious smile.

"What a great idea. Come on, Dimitri. We have a movie date."

Ivanna takes off, leaving Dimitri behind. He sighs. "That was evil, Lia. Pure evil."

Her eyes narrow on his. "You deserve every minute of it, too. Now go be a good lackey and watch my best friend."

He huffs, taking off after Ivanna.

NIKOLAI

Clearing my throat, I look down at Lia.

"You ready to go?"

She sighs. "It doesn't really matter, now does it."

Instead of responding, I lead her out the door to the waiting car. Anton is standing at the door, opening when we approach.

I help Lia inside, sliding in beside her when she moves over for me. Once we are settled, Anton gets into the passenger seat as the driver starts the journey to the club.

"We need to talk, Lia."

She looks over at me, her eyes blank. When she doesn't speak, I continue.

"We are going to Club Atlas. Do you know what that is?"

She shakes her head no.

"It's a sex club run by the Polish Mafia. I'm bringing you as my guest. With that being said, women are viewed differently in this club. They are considered pets. You will be expected to be demure and only speak when spoken to."

She clears her throat. "Will you let them touch me?"

I growl at the thought of anyone touching my *kroshka*.

"They will only touch you if I allow it. Follow the rules and you will be safe."

I don't mean the words I speak. I won't let anyone touch her, but ever since the trust between us has shattered, I've had to resort to extreme measures to keep her in line.

If it wasn't for her safety, I would never try to control her like this. The way she mouths off to me is sexy as fuck.

The men at this club won't feel the same. They would demand a whipping if she speaks to me the way she does at home.

"Understood," she says, her eyes going back to the window.

Reaching over, I grab her hand. She startles, trying to pull back. I grip her tighter.

"I will be touching you tonight, Felicity. You will see things you won't like, but I need you to trust me."

She scoffs. "I trusted you once. That's how I ended up branded like cattle."

Leaning into her ear, I hiss at her, "I've never thought of you as cattle. That brand is a layer of protection only."

She swallows hard. "Can we not do this? I've already told you I will behave. What else is left to say?"

I swallow back a retort, giving her the silence she demands. Pulling back from her, I keep her hand, but settle into my seat.

Neither one of us speaks again until we arrive at the club.

"When we get out of this car, I will be cold and ruthless. Don't take anything I say personally. You need to stay by my side at all times and keep your head down. Understood?"

She lets out a humorless laugh. "Other than clinging to you, it'll be just like we are at home."

I go to chastise her for her words, but the door opens suddenly.

I step out, extending my hand inside to help her out. Once she is on her feet, she tucks closer to my side, her arm sliding into the crook of my elbow.

Keeping her head down, she relies on me to lead her. I have to admit, the blind trust she is placing in me is heady. I want to drown in this feeling, but seeing the door ahead, I focus my mind on the game we are about to play.

I rarely come to Club Atlas. I don't enjoy the sex club environment, but that's not why. This isn't only a sex club. It's a front for his operations. Many of the women inside these walls are victims of human trafficking, and there is nothing I can do about it. This is his territory, not mine.

Still, seeing the women walking around naked as they serve their masters makes me pull Lia in closer to me.

"Nikolai. What a pleasure. I am so glad you reached out," the leader of the Polish says as he approaches.

I nod. "It has been too long, Jakub. How have you been?"

He opens his hands, gesturing around him. "Amazing. Flourishing as usual. What about you?"

"Same, my friend."

His eyes flick to the girl at my side. I made sure to position her so her brand would be facing him, immediately showing him who she is to me.

"I didn't realize you were partaking. I thought you banned pets in your area," he muses as he eyes her brand.

I smirk at him. "Do you really think the rules apply to me? I'm the leader. If I want a pet, I will have one."

"Does your pet have a name?"

I let my smile grow. "Of course, but it doesn't matter. It's pet now. Isn't that right?"

I nip at her ear. She withholds a yelp, nodding instead.

"She's very well trained. Did you do it yourself?" he asks, sounding impressed.

"Of course."

"Well, I would love to hear more about it. How about we move to my personal VIP area?"

"That sounds wonderful."

Following Jakub, I guide Lia through the main area of the club. All around us, people are getting a show. On the stages, women are being whipped and beaten. Some are being fucked by multiple men. Then there are the men at the tables being ridden or getting their cocks sucked.

I never understood why a man would want to sit at a table with another man and get his cock sucked. I mean, some of them continue on their business as if there isn't a woman slobbering on his knob. I mean, it's disgraceful.

Still, I have to keep my head in the game, so I continue on. Not letting my feelings show.

When we finally reach the VIP area, I chose to sit in the chair opposite of Jakub, pulling Lia into my lap. I let my hand linger between her legs, sliding up until it's just under the hem of her dress.

I can feel her tense, but otherwise, she lays her head on my shoulder, keeping her eyes down.

After giving our orders to a passing woman, Jakub focuses on Lia again.

"She's a gorgeous one. Where did you find her?"

I chuckle. "She stumbled right into my compound. Seems she was being mistreated by her foster parent and thought my walls would save her. Little did she know, she walked right into the devil's den."

I watch as his eyes flash with the information.

Yeah, I know Charles is your man. This is the girl he let get the best of him. You move next.

Jakub clears his throat. "A lucky devil you are. She's prime real estate. I could make a small fortune off of her at market. Is she still intact?"

I barely withhold the growl threatening to come out. Thankfully, the woman comes back, handing me my vodka, giving me a second to compose myself.

I scoff. "Of course not. I've been snacking on her like a fiend."

He tsks his tongue. "Too bad. The virgins make a killing."

"I'm sure, but my pet isn't for sale. I'm not done breaking her yet."

He nods. "So what do I owe the pleasure then, if not to broker a sale of your pet?"

"I've been told that my uncle is under the impression that I am no longer fit to lead. The whispers claim you are his main benefactor. As you know, my father left the throne to me. I am here to see the validity of the claim and to possibly broker a new deal between the Russians and Polish."

He pauses a moment. "I know nothing of your uncle's plans. He only visits when he wants to partake in some meat, but I would be willing to hear out a proposal for an alliance. What did you have in mind?" he lies smoothly.

I watch as his eyes flicker, a telltale sign he's hiding something. I already know of his ties with my uncle, so that was only a test.

"What are your needs? Maybe we can come to a mutual understanding."

I already know what he is going to ask for. The answer is no, but I need to get him talking.

"I don't need anything, but opening up the line through your territory would ease some of the logistics and line both of our pockets. That is, if your stance on the situation has changed."

I purse my lips, stroking the inside of Lia's legs to calm myself. The hand she has on the back of my neck caresses the skin, helping the tension ease.

"I would be willing to look into it. At the time I made that decision, I was in a bad place to make such drastic decisions. I've now found that I need to reevaluate them and move on with the future. Who would you suggest as a liaison?"

He smiles. "Jan on the Polish side. Since he's already here so often, Oleg may be your best bet on your side."

Gotcha.

No one would want Oleg as the liaison. He's an old, deceitful man. He must already be receiving a cut from Jakub. Doing it this way, I would owe that cut to Oleg instead of Jakub, making him more money.

"That is an idea. I'm not sure I can trust him with the job, though. His attentions would be elsewhere." I let my eyes roam the women walking around.

"Yes, he does enjoy playing, but I would make sure the nights he is here on business, that he is strictly professional."

"Still, he is getting up there in age. You think he can still handle the game?" I ask, tilting my head to the side, looking like I'm thinking about it.

"Of course. Age is only a number. It is all about your spirit. He has plenty of that."

Dig your hole deeper.

"Very well. I will take it into consideration."

After a moment, he speaks up again. "Since business is concluded, might I request an hour with your pet?"

I grip Lia's thigh, not willing to let her go.

CHAPTER SIXTEEN

Lia

"Since business is concluded, might I request an hour with your pet?"

My blood freezes.

So far, all I've done is listen to the disgusting things Nikolai has spit since we got here. The most I've had to deal with is some leering and Nikolai's hand on my thigh.

My stomach rolls at the thought of this man touching me.

Nikolai's hand tightens between my legs.

"I don't like to share. Maybe when I'm finished with her."

I let out the breath I didn't realize I was holding. He has kept his word to protect me as long as I behave.

The man laughs quietly. "What a shame. Well, if that's it for business, I think I will go find my own brunette beauty to brutalize. Feel free to use any of the rooms."

Nikolai smiles. "Thank you, my friend."

I don't know if the man has left or not, but Nikolai stays seated. After a moment, he moves me until I am straddling his lap.

Leaning in, he grabs my hair, pulling my ear to his lips. "Alright, *kroshka*. It's time to give them a show. They are watching my every move. Let's show them what a good girl you can be."

His hand tightens in my hair as he brings his lips to mine. I hiss at the pain, but the sound is lost as he opens his mouth over mine. His tongue demands entrance, which I give him easily.

At first, I'm aware of our surroundings, nervous about what he meant by us being watched, but the more he strokes his tongue against mine, the more I lose myself.

By the time his hands start to caress my body, I'm totally lost to him. Even if I wanted to, I couldn't stop.

My hips grind against him without abandon. This dress did not allow for panties, so my bare pussy rubs against his slacks, creating the perfect friction. By the time I'm soaring toward an orgasm, he pulls away, his breaths coming harder.

"I'm going to do something, and you are going to take it."

His demanding tone heats my body.

"Yes, sir," I say, louder than I planned.

He smirks at me, reaching between us to unbutton his pants.

My nerves start to get the better of me when he pulls himself out. I'm still a virgin and I do not want to lose it here and now. Still, my body wants to obey him.

Nikolai grips one hip, pulling me closer to him while his other hand holds his dick away from my center. Once my heat is against his, he moves his other hand to my other hip.

"Grind on me, *kroshka*. Make yourself come," he grunts.

I don't hesitate. The feel of his skin against my clit is driving me insane. I gyrate my hips against him, his cock sliding between my lips, stroking my clit the way I need. The idea that one wrong move would have him slipping inside me is both erotic and nerve-racking, but before I can get lost in my thoughts, Nikolai takes charge.

Leaning forward, he latches on to my breast through the material of my dress. Pinching my nipple between his teeth, I let out a loud moan of approval. My hips move faster against his as I feel the tightness build up inside. At this point, I wouldn't care if the pope was standing next to me. I'm chasing that high.

Nikolai buries his hand in my hair, jerking my head back so he has access to my throat. As soon as he latches on to it, sucking and biting, I explode. I can feel the wetness between my legs drip all over him as my body continues to jerk against him.

He doesn't stop sucking until my body stills.

He smiles against my skin, kissing the spot once.

"My good girl," he whispers before tucking himself back into his pants.

Then he helps me stand, which I'm grateful for when my knees give out. He holds me against his chest as he straightens my dress before moving us back through the club. Jakub meets us at the door, a smile on his face.

"You let her orgasm. What a kindness," Jakub tells Nikolai.

Nikolai only smirks. "You asked how I trained her. Rewards and punishment work well. Such a quiet pet tonight. Coveted by all the men around us." He leans in, kissing my neck again. "She earned a reward."

"Whatever you say. I prefer straight punishments. Fear does something to their body. It's one hell of an experience."

Nikolai strokes my hip, over my brand. "I'll have to try it. Now if you'll excuse me, I have another matter to attend to."

"I look forward to hearing from you soon."

"You as well."

Nikolai escorts me from the club and into the back seat. We are quiet the entire way home, but my body is humming. I want to be upset that he forced that upon me in such a public arena, but the other part is getting hot over the idea that there were eyes on us the entire time.

By the time we make it back to the house, I'm ready to climb Nikolai like a tree if it means this ache in my center goes away.

Nikolai has other plans. As soon as we made it through the door, he turned to Anton. "Escort Felicity to her room and inform Maxim he is on duty."

"Nikolai?" I ask as he starts to walk away.

He turns, looking at me, the distance back in his eye. "Go to bed."

With that, he leaves me standing there in the foyer, turned on and confused as hell.

"Come on, Miss Lia."

I give Anton a small smile as I follow him, but my mind can't stop thinking about the night.

What the fuck was that about?

NIK

Walking down the hall toward my study, I hear something hit the floor with a thud and a soft muttered curse. I stop outside the door and see Lia standing up on her tippy toes, trying to reach a book above her head. Without a thought, I walk up behind her, pressing my body against hers.

"This one?" I rasp, hand hovering over a spine.

"Yes, please," she says as she presses back into me.

It's almost as if her actions are natural, her mind not connecting with her body. I know she's still mad at me, but I can tell she is slowly forgiving me too.

She started eating dinner with us again. Ever since the meeting at the club, she has even given me a smile or two.

I drop one hand to her hips and hold her against me as I reach for the book.

"Here," I say as I pull it off the shelf, handing it to her.

"Thank you," she says softly before setting it down on a shelf she can reach.

Lia turns in my arms, resting her hands on my chest.

"Studying again?"

"I am."

I watch as her little tongue peeks out as she licks her bottom lip as she stares at mine.

"Have something on your mind, *kroshka?*"

"I have no idea what you're talking about," she says as she sways into me.

I duck my head as she comes in close, lips barely touching. Just as I move in to kiss her, my phone starts ringing, making Lia jump, pulling away.

"Ouch," she says, rubbing the back of her head from hitting the bookshelf.

I hesitate, not wanting this moment to end. This is the first time she has initiated a kiss with me. Knowing that it's come after the breach of trust between us, makes me want to cherish it.

The phone stops ringing only to immediately start up again.

"Yeah, you better answer that." Her voice is soft, but there is resolve back in her eyes.

The moment has passed.

Reaching into my pocket, I pull out my phone and see it's Banya. They wouldn't be calling unless there's an issue.

"Yeah?" I answer.

"Sir, your uncle is here and we have an issue," the person on the other end says.

"I'm on my way," I say as I step back from Lia.

As I hang up, she grabs the book, clutching it to her chest. I shoot off a text to the driver letting him know to meet me outside before dropping my phone back into my pocket.

"I'll see you later. Have fun studying," I say as I walk away.

She doesn't respond, making me shake my head. I was so close.

As I approach the front door, Dimitri walks out of the kitchen.

"Where are you going?" he asks.

"I need to go to Banya. Oleg is causing issues."

"Do you need me to come with you?" he asks, stepping forward.

I shake my head. "Stay here with the girls. If I need you, I'll call."

"Sounds good."

"We will talk when I get back," I say as I open the door. I walk outside and see the driver pulling up.

Once he comes to a stop, I get in. "Go to Banya," I tell him before pressing the button, putting the divider up.

As he drives, I check my email, seeing if there is anything that needs my attention now. I see an email from Haruaki Takahashi making sure that there are no hard feelings. He has taken over for his father, meaning he would be reaching out to make contact with anyone his father dealt with. While I have transported weapons for them in the past, I haven't worked for him in a while. Still, he may be worried I would retaliate for the slight against Ivan.

I type out a quick response advising that there were no repercussions from our chapter. I wished him well with his takeover before I hit send.

As soon as we pull up to Banya, I get out of the car and march up to the door.

"I'm so sorry, I didn't know what to do," the scared worker says as soon as I step inside. I ignore her and walk right past her.

I move through the hall, past the showers, into the plunge pool area. I stop when the body comes into view, floating face down.

"Where is he?" I grit out.

"He's in the sauna, sir," one of the men says as he steps forward.

"Fish him out," I say, pointing toward the body before I take off.

I hear his laughter before I see him. Opening the door, I see him sitting on a bench with the felt hat on his head, and a towel around his waist as someone swats the venik on his back as he drinks his tea.

"You are overdressed," he says as I step inside, my shirt instantly sticking to me thanks to the humidity.

"Why is there a body floating in the plunge pool?" I ask.

Oleg takes his time responding, pouring more water over the rocks, creating more steam.

"He stuck his nose where it didn't belong. So I took care of it." He shrugs.

"We do not go killing others without reason, especially without my permission. Something in which you did not have," I say calmly despite the throbbing in my temples.

"Your father wouldn't have opposed."

"Family or not, you must follow the rules. Do you understand?"

Oleg looks at me thoughtfully before nodding. "As you wish."

"As this is your first offense" —where he was caught at least— "your next two payments from the account will be suspended. If a second offense is made, a physical payment will be required."

He bows his head slightly. I should shoot him dead now, but his connections would be lost. I really need Dimitri to take them over sooner rather than later.

Turning, I step out of the sauna and make my way back through the bathhouse.

"His body will be picked up within the hour. In the meantime, I will put it in the maintenance room out of sight," the man says as he fishes the body out of the pool.

"Keep me updated," I say as I pass.

Once I reach the front desk, I stop, resting my hands on the counter. "Please let me know when he leaves."

"Of course." She nods.

I tap the desk and make my way out. I get into the car and pull out my phone, hitting his number. It rings three times before he answers.

"I need you to pull up the cameras for Banya. He killed a man in the pool and I want to know why."

"I'll have the information to you within the hour," Alexei says before hanging up.

I lean my head back against the headrest as the driver starts to weave through traffic and take a deep breath.

How much more can I take?

CHAPTER SEVENTEEN

NIK

"Alexei has an update on Oleg." Dimitri pulls my attention away from the screen in front of me.

Anytime Lia is out on the practice grounds, I try to watch her. She's made tremendous progress.

Today, she is out there with Maxim and Anton. The men know to go easy on the girls, but they still spar with them.

Part of me wants to snap every limb in their body when they touch Lia, but I know it's what's best. She's back refusing to acknowledge me. The woman has had so many mood swings, I feel like I have whiplash.

Giving Dimitri my full attention, I ask, "What is it?"

"He seems to be assembling a group of men. Alexei is identifying them and putting them on a roster for us. So far, it's a mix of Polish and our men. No one that has been on site though. The man from Banya was one of our foot soldiers he was attempting to sway to his side. The man decided to stay loyal to us and lost his life."

I nod. "Does he know what it's for?"

He shakes his head. "It has been hush-hush, from what he can tell. He's digging deeper into the computer files he could get his hands on. He is going to let us know when they move."

"You think we should be ready to counterattack?"

"That would be my move," Dimitri tells me honestly.

"Very well. Get a group of men together. Leave Maxim and Anton on Ivanna and Felicity. I want them in the house before we leave."

"You want me to stay behind?" Dimitri offers.

I know he hates me being out there without him, but he hates leaving Ivanna more.

"I need you with me on this one. You will lead the men should I fall."

"Got it, boss."

Moving out of my office, I head into the study. Opening the safe room, I head to the far wall, opening our armory.

"What do you think is going on?" I ask Dimitri, wanting to know his gut feeling.

"It's not good. I don't know where his head is at, but it's not good. The fact that he has Polish men with him tells me your show at the club didn't go over the way we had hoped."

I grunt. "He felt I was too soft for allowing her to orgasm."

Dimitri's eyes widen. "You didn't tell me you fucked her."

I shake my head. "I didn't, but I made it appear that we were. He wanted a show. I gave him the only one I was willing to give."

"It might have blown your cover."

I shrug. "I was never considering his offer, anyway. It wouldn't have mattered. He was already working with Oleg. Where do you think he will attack?"

"He won't come here. We are fortified, and he would lose most of his men. My best guess would be to hit you where it will hurt. Oleg knows you prefer to visit Banya most often. My guess is he will hit there. It's one of our biggest stash places and brings in decent money," Dimitri says thoughtfully.

I roll the idea over in my head. It would be a smart move. One my father would have done. Oleg did take many notes from the man, but he's also slightly more in control of his emotions than my father was.

"Dispatch the men there. I want the girls back in this house within ten minutes. Then we leave."

"On it."

After he leaves, I look back at the wall in front of me. Taking down a couple of guns, several knives, and even a grenade, I start suiting up.

Still, the more ready I get, the more I have a nagging feeling that something isn't right. I'm missing something.

When Dimitri returns, he advises me the girls are in Ivanna's room. After I'm all ready, I leave Dimitri to let him suit up.

Knocking on the door, I step inside to find the girls with Maxim and Anton talking over their training.

"Give us a moment," I tell the guys.

They nod, stepping out. Moving closer to the girls, I kneel in front of where they sit on the edge of the bed.

"What's wrong?" Lia asks as Ivanna reaches over, grabbing her hand.

"I don't know what is about to go down. You both remember how to get into the safe room, correct?"

They nod.

"Good. Do you have your knives?"

Ivanna smiles, holding hers up. Lia frowns. "I dropped mine off in my room when I grabbed a change of clothes."

Reaching into my boot, I pull one out. "Here. Take mine. Remember that we are not one hundred percent sure who to trust, so trust your gut."

"What's going on?" Lia asks.

I reach forward, cupping her face. For once, she lets me without complaint.

"My uncle is making his move. We are trying to anticipate it, but there is no way to be sure. So if there is an attack here, get to the safe room as quickly as possible and stay there. If you run into anyone, stab first, ask questions later. Your number one priority is staying alive."

She nods. Leaning forward, I press a quick kiss to her lips. Then I turn to Ivanna and kiss her head.

"You stay safe too, kid. Take care of my girl here."

Ivanna chuckles. "Just go. We will be fine here. Besides, we have Maxim and Anton. They will protect us with their life."

"They better or else they will face my wrath."

"Go on. If you want to lose Dimitri while you're out there, I wouldn't mind," Ivanna jokes.

"This isn't a joke, Ivanna. If I lose him, it means he will be dead. Do you really want that?"

She shakes her head, losing all humor. "Of course not. You both will come back fine. You're both too stubborn to die."

Shaking my head, I stand. Lia reaches out, squeezing my hand.

"We have our disagreements, but stay safe," she says carefully.

I give her a curt nod, leaving them behind. Once outside the door, I turn to the two men that I'm leaving as guards.

"You have both proved your loyalty. You protect them with your lives. Remember, there is a traitor in our midst. Don't trust anyone, but Dimitri or me."

Once they both agree, I take off toward the front door. Dimitri meets me there.

"You ready, boss?"

"As ready as I'll ever be."

Lia

"Gosh, this is so boring. I hate being locked up." Ivanna has moved on from watching the movie we put on to complaining about life. As she starts to belt out Akon's "Locked Up," I chuckle.

We have been in the entertainment room for three hours waiting for news from the guys. Seems one and a half movies is all Ivanna has in her.

"You should have been in theater. You are such a drama queen."

"I'm being serious. The guys are out there fighting for our lives while we sit here, waiting for them to return. Not that I want to be there. I'm sure whatever they are doing is dangerous as fuck, but you get what I mean. We have been on lockdown for months now. There is legitimately nothing else I want to watch," she whines.

I'm about to respond when I hear something outside.

"Did you hear that?" I ask, body tensing.

"What? My body slowly dying from inactivity?"

"No. Shh. Listen."

I hear it again. A couple of grunts, almost like a fight.

Standing, I make my way over to where we left Maxim and Anton.

"What's going on outside?"

Maxim gives me a quizzical look. "What do you mean?"

My gut is telling me something is very wrong. Turning to Ivanna, I say, "Let's go hang out in the safe room."

She rolls her eyes. "Sure. An actual cage. Why not."

Before we can step out of the room, shattering glass echoes behind us. I scream, grabbing Ivanna's arm to pull her down the hall. Maxim already has his gun out, shooting into the room.

"Take the girls to the safe room," he tells Anton.

I look behind us to see Maxim entering the entertainment room. I send up a quick prayer that he is okay. Maxim has become a close friend to me. one of the few people in this world I feel I can actually trust.

Anton's running behind us, pushing us forward, but before we make it to the library, a man steps out.

Anton raises a gun, shooting at the man, but he ducks, evading the attack. Anton grabs my arm, jerking me into the door next to us. Only my firm grip on Ivanna clues her into our movements. She is focused on the attacker, ready to fight.

After he slams it shut behind us, he locks it.

"Go," he hisses, ushering us down the dark stairs.

"What are we doing? I can take him," she hisses at Anton.

He nudges her forward again. "This isn't a game. My main objective is to get you to safety. Now move your ass."

Ivanna grunts, but makes her way down the stairs. I hold on to her back, staying with her the entire way. She might be willing to try out her skills on these men, but I know I won't be able to hold my own. My training has been centered on self-defense. The end goal has always been to escape the situation, not stand there and attempt to fight to the end. I can feel my body tremble as we make our way through the dark.

"Grab on to me and keep up," Anton says as he brushes past us to take the lead.

Stepping forward, I grab him, pulling Ivanna up to grab him as well. My nerves are shot at this point. The basement is dark and dank. Every little noise I hear makes me flinch. Especially when I hear the door we came through splinter.

Anton moves faster, likely hearing the same thing I did. He stops suddenly, moving to push an item out of the way. What he reveals is a dimly lit tunnel.

"This will take us out to the practice fields. From there, I will get you to a safe house."

Nodding, we follow him.

I look back over my shoulder, waiting to see someone chasing us, but it never comes. By the time the entrance to the basement fades from view, my heart calms a little.

My thoughts start to wander then, wondering what happened to Maxim. I have to believe he will be okay. I have to believe they will all be okay.

Nikolai and Dimitri are out there somewhere too. Nikolai warned that something bad might happen. Why didn't he stay with us?

Shaking the thought, I shoot another prayer up that we all make it out of this alive.

Once we reach the end of the tunnel, Anton helps us climb up a ladder.

My gut is screaming at me, but at this point, I don't know which part of tonight it is worried about. I mean, we have already been ambushed.

Still, that little voice in the back of my head is wondering why the man who was breaking into the basement never caught up. Could he have encountered another guard? Maybe Maxim? Is he dead now? And why are we leaving? We were supposed to go to the safe room, not a safe house.

Once I clear the hole, an arm wraps around me, a hand clamped over my mouth. I attempt to fight, but the rough fingers latch on to my nose as well, taking my breath from me. My hands reach up, digging into the unknown attacker's skin, but whoever it is doesn't even falter. If anything, the grip becomes tighter.

My vision blurs, black dots multiplying with each blink. My chest aches as I try to gulp in air. I'm slowly losing consciousness when I see Ivanna's blonde hair poke out of the hole.

Internally, I'm screaming at her to look up. To jump back down and run as fast as she can. She doesn't though.

The last thing I remember is Ivanna's wide eyes as she meets mine. She had been saying something, but a man steps in behind her, grabbing her much like I was grabbed. Right before my world goes black, I see her elbow the man.

My last thought before I lose myself to the dark chasm is about her.

I hope you make it, Ivanna.

CHAPTER EIGHTEEN

NIK

We arrive at Banya, and all is quiet. I rendezvous with my team before setting up, ready for an attack. Oleg doesn't disappoint. Three hours later, he shows up, full army and all. Bullets fly before a word can be spoken.

After about fifteen minutes of constant fire, his side stops suddenly.

"Something's not right," I tell Dimitri.

"You're right."

After a few moments of silence, I call out, "Where's Oleg? Your fearless leader sent you into battle and is not willing to even fight by your side? Is that the type of man you want to follow?"

No one speaks.

I scoff. "I never send my men into battle alone. If the cause is worth dying for, then I'm the first on the front line. I know some of you are Polish and for you, I ask you to go back to your leader. You have no business being part of this. As for the Russians, this is a one-time offer. If you defer back to your true leader, your lives will be spared."

One man chuckles then. "You are weak. You would let traitors live? Is that how the Russians run their Bratva? Pitiful. No wonder your men willingly left you."

"It is not a weakness to see the way my uncle has poisoned these men with lies. I only offer them another future. Senseless death accomplishes nothing."

The man only laughs louder. "Keep giving your life lessons." He looks at his watch. "We have distracted you long enough. End them so we can go see the prizes we collected tonight. I have dibs on the brunette that likes to ride Russian cock."

I growl, aiming and shooting the man in the head. Cocky fucker didn't expect that.

Next thing I know, we are back in a firefight.

"They are at the house," I hiss at Dimitri.

"I got that. I tried calling Maxim and Anton, but got nothing. All we can do is end this quick and get back there. I'm sure the girls are fine."

I take a deep breath. I want to believe his words, but I have a feeling this was all a setup. Oleg isn't here. Instead, he is probably at my house, taking my girl and my sister.

Fuck.

It takes thirty more minutes to flush all their men out. We leave not one of them alive. I task one soldier with collecting their phones while Dimitri and I rush back to the house. When we arrive, my heart sinks.

There is not a window still intact. Most of the men are dead and the ones that aren't are gravely injured.

We search the entire house, not finding a trace of the girls. The log on the safe room shows they never made it there. However, when I watch back the footage, I find Anton leading them into the basement.

My heart is filled with hope. Maybe he got them out and to safety and hasn't had a chance to contact us yet.

Racing downstairs and through the tunnels, I pause when I find Maxim crawling.

"Maxim? What happened?"

He turns over, lying on his back.

"Sneak attack. Whoever is their inside man was here tonight. They helped them slip past without alerting us. I watched Anton bring the girls down here. I attempted to follow, but ran into that asshole back there," he grits out.

I look down at his leg, seeing it bent in an awkward position. "It's broken. Lie here. I will call the doctor for you. I need to find her."

"Go. Don't waste a second on me. She's the priority."

I grip his shoulder, showing my thanks as I take off.

Racing to the end of the tunnel, I climb out to find the area desolate. Not a single sign that anyone was here.

Picking up my phone, I try Anton again, but get nothing. He could have lost it in battle, but he should have checked in by now.

By the time I make it back to Dimitri, he has Maxim up, helping to support his way as he pulls the man back to the house. I take up his other side, focusing on getting him up the stairs and into the main living area before I start barking out my orders.

"Dimitri, call Alexei. Tell him I want every little thing he has on my uncle. I want to know if he has the girls. After that, walk the property and bring any injured back here. Call in a couple of guys back to help." He nods, taking off, then I turn to Maxim. "Did Dimitri call the doctor?"

"Yes. He is on his way," he grits through his teeth.

"Good. Now tell me everything."

"Anton and I were standing watch outside the entertainment room while the girls watched movies. It was quiet. Then Lia ran out saying she heard noises outside. I was about to go check it out when two assailants crashed through the window. I told the girls to run and ordered Anton to stick with them at all costs. By the time I fought off the two men, they were gone. I went to search for them and make sure they made it to the safe room, but when I passed the basement, I noticed the door open. At the entrance to the tunnel, a man stood, almost as if on guard. He's the one that broke my leg. I strangled him before trying to make my way down the tunnel. I don't know what happened to Anton, but the way the man was guarding the tunnel makes me think that there was someone on the other end. Someone who knew about the tunnel and had planned on us using it."

A grim feeling settles over me. Anton is most likely dead then. Or…

"Do you think Anton could be the traitor?" I say slowly, dread filling my gut.

Maxim thinks it over. "I want to say no because I've known the man for five years, but at this point, I wouldn't trust anyone. If I were you, I would even be questioning mine and Dimitri's loyalty. Your main goal needs to be getting the girls back."

"I appreciate your candor. I'm going to get them back. Wait here for the doctor."

I leave him sitting in the room to go find Dimitri. It doesn't take long. I find him at the front gate, coordinating search and rescue efforts for our men.

"Line all the dead against this wall. We will want to honor our men while also noting the families we will take care of. Any that are left alive, bring them to the house for medical care. If you feel they are too far gone, you have permission to show mercy. As for the attackers, line them up over there." He points away from where our men will be. "I will take fingerprints and search them myself when you're done. Any questions?"

The men shake their heads.

"Good. Report with anything suspicious. We have two girls missing. Keep an eye and ear out. You're dismissed."

Once they all disperse, I turn to Dimitri. "Anton should have checked in by now. He's either dead or a traitor. Have you heard from Alexei yet?"

"He said he was going to get closer, whatever that means. He told me he would call me within an hour. If I don't hear from him, his phone will auto send me his coordinates so we can find him."

"I don't like this," I tell him, dread settling in my stomach.

Something isn't right. I need to be doing something.

"You think I do? I should have stayed here. Ivanna is my responsibility. If anything happens to her, I…" he trails off.

"I know. I feel the same."

We are silent a moment, each lost in our own minds when his phone rings.

"Tell me you have something," he asks as soon as he answers. His voice sounds desperate.

After a moment of listening, he curses before speaking. "Good work. Let me know if you hear anything else."

"What is it?" I ask as soon as he hangs up.

"Jakub is having a special auction at Club Atlas tonight. Seems he has two new girls that have been marked as unique and highly coveted."

"Fuck. That's got to be them. Did he say if Oleg was with them?"

"He said Oleg never left his home earlier. As far as he's aware, he is still there. What do you want to do?"

I pace, considering our next step. "Oleg never planned for me to die at that gunfight. He knew he couldn't win. That's why he wasn't there. The whole thing was a setup to get us out of the house. He wants Felicity. My only question is why would he turn around and sell her? I've seen the way he looks at her. The comments he has made. He wants to defile her before selling her as a 'fuck you' to me. He must not know that Jakub has changed the plan."

"You think Jakub's crossed him?"

"Oh, I know he did. He doesn't need Oleg. I believe he entertained him as a little game. The man loves playing with his prey first. My best guess is that he planned to take Oleg out himself after I was dealt with, but Felicity stepped in the way. From there, he has been adapting."

"Then you took her into his club and flaunted her," he says, following my train of thought.

"He fixated on her as a prize. I bet they didn't even plan to take Ivanna until she showed up at the end of that tunnel with Felicity."

"So what do we do?"

"I'm going to call my uncle and inform him of this betrayal. See what kind of shit we can kick up. Then we are going to get our girls back."

Picking up my phone, I dial Oleg's number.

After two rings, he answers, "You're still alive. What a pity."

I laugh at his casual response. "It takes more than a couple of two-bit gangsters to kill me, dear uncle."

"Yes, it was unlikely, yet I still hoped a stray bullet would do the dirty deed. Still, the evening was successful. Tell me, nephew, are you missing anything?"

"Oh, I am, but I know exactly where they are. The question is, do you?"

"She will be delivered to me shortly."

She. Singular. He doesn't know they took Ivanna.

"I can guarantee that neither Ivanna nor Felicity will be delivered to you. My spies have them at Club Atlas for a special auction for only the best customers. Since you didn't receive an invitation, I can assume you are not considered special enough."

"What? You're lying," he says with an edge of panic.

I only laugh harder. "You thought you could win by partnering with the Polish, but you only dug a deeper hole. They will never let you live. I'm sure they have men on their way to murder you now. Do try to make it through the night. I'd prefer to watch the light fade from your eyes myself."

I hang up before he can respond.

"What's next, boss?" Dimitri asks.

"Next, we go to war."

Lia

Why does my head hurt?

Slowly, I blink my eyes open but shut them as soon as the light hits them. I feel like what I assume a hangover would feel like, but I've never had one. I never drink. I hate feeling out of control.

So what happened?

I try to think back in my head, but it only makes the pounding more intense.

Groaning, I turn over, feeling across the bed for my phone.

I frown when I realize I'm not on a bed. I'm on a concrete floor.

Fuck. What the fuck happened?

Nausea rolls through my stomach when I attempt to open my eyes again.

Shake it off, Lia. You have to open your eyes.

Taking a couple of deep breaths, I open my eyes again, forcing them to remain open as I take in the surroundings.

Nikolai

I have to blink often, but after a few minutes, my eyes adjust. Slowly, I try to sit up, gagging a couple of times from the pain splitting through my head. It takes forever, but finally, I prop myself against the wall I was lying next to.

Opening my eyes again, I have a better handle on myself. The room I'm in is empty other than a bucket in the corner. There are no windows. Only a closed door.

I try to remember again what happened, but it's coming back in fragments.

I remember Nikolai pressing a kiss to my lips. The worry I felt for him and wanting him to stay with me.

What I don't remember is why. Why was I so worried?

Closing my eyes, I replay the kiss.

Nikolai pressing his lips to mine. He's telling me something. What is he trying to tell me? To be safe. Keep safe. He's leaving. Why is he leaving? Something's happening. Maxim and Anton.

I gasp as another memory hits.

Maxim standing at the door of the entertainment room, gun in hand, as he yells for us to get to the safe room.

We were attacked at the house. We were running. Why aren't we in the safe room? Where is Ivanna?

After several minutes of trying to force myself to remember more, I take a break. All it did was make my head hurt more.

Suddenly, the door is flung open as a man drags Ivanna inside. She's attempting to fight him, but her hands are cuffed behind her back. She has on a see-through negligee, which is not like her at all.

"Stop fighting, bitch." The man tosses her down.

Then he points at me. "Don't try anything stupid. I'll be back for you."

He looks down at his arm, cussing at the blood flowing before backing out of the room.

I look over at Ivanna, blood on her lips. "Are you okay?"

She chuckles. "I'm fine. His arm is going to hurt like a bitch, though. Are you okay?"

I swallow hard. "My head feels like it was hit by a truck and anytime I move I feel like I'm about to puke."

She nods. "It's the drugs. After you passed out, they injected you with something. They were going to do the same with me, but I agreed to cooperate. The only reason that asshole got bit was because he groped my boobs."

I frown at her. "Why would you agree to cooperate?"

She rolls her eyes. "One of us had to stay conscious. We need a plan to get out of here."

"What? You should have saved yourself. Why didn't you run?"

She shakes her head. "I would never leave you to fend for yourself. You're my best friend. If you are up the creek without a paddle, bitch, I'm right next to you, helping you claw your way out of it. That's how this works."

My eyes tear up. "You really are amazing. Do you think the guys know we are gone yet?"

She shrugs. "No way of knowing. We don't even know where they were going. No point in relying on them. We need our own plan."

Taking a deep breath, I focus. "Okay, so what do we do?"

She smiles. "I knew you were tough. Alright, so I have figured out that we are at Club Atlas. You've been here before, right?"

"Only in the VIP area with Nikolai. I kept my head down, so I don't know how helpful that will be," I confirm.

"That's okay. So asshole there, let it slip that there is an auction tonight and I'm the main attraction, hence the outfit. My guess is that you are too, since he said he was coming back for you. We need to get out of here before we make it to that point. When he was leading me back, he wasn't as careful as he was when he took me away from here. The room he cleaned me up in was at the end of the hall to the left, but I heard a door open and some chatter the opposite way. I believe that is our way out. What do you think?"

"I mean, you have more experience with this, so I trust you. How do we get there? I mean you are handcuffed."

She laughs. "Handcuffs are nothing. I can get out of these in a heartbeat. The real question is, when do we make a move and how do we get out undetected?"

My mind mulls over the question. If the chatter she heard was from the club, we may be able to pose as one of the girls who works here. I think back to that night. I remember the girl who leaned over to give Nikolai his drink. She was nude. So if we do it, we need to be nude to avoid detection. We may have to be willing to be touched.

Can I do that?

If it means living, I think I can.

I look down at myself. I'm filthy. Dirt mars my skin. That won't do.

"I'll go with him and get cleaned up. When he comes back, we make our move," I tell Ivanna.

She nods. "Good idea. It gives me time to plan a way to knock him out. We can grab his gun and keys."

I shake my head. "We can grab it, but if we make it to the door, we will need to ditch it along with our clothes. The servers are naked. If we try to blend with them, we can make it to the back and get out of here."

"That's not a bad idea. I don't like the thought of being without a weapon, but okay, let's do it."

"If you think of anything better while I'm gone, I'm down. I will also keep an eye out when he takes me."

We sit in silence a moment, then Ivanna speaks up. "We are going to be okay. You know that, right?"

Rolling my shoulders, I ignore the restless feeling inside of me. "Of course we are. We are going to make it out alive and laugh about this in a couple of months. That's after Dimitri becomes even more overbearing to you and Nikolai tans my ass for letting you get captured."

She snorts. "He will be furious that we both got taken."

I shake my head. "I'm expendable. He might enjoy letting me warm his bed, but at the end of the day, if you weren't with me, I don't believe he would attempt to save me."

My heart aches with the honest admission. I've been pushing them down for so long, but sitting here now, I realize I was living a fantasy. Letting myself be okay with accepting only a part of Nikolai, when the truth is I want his everything. Something he will never be able to offer me.

"You're wrong, Lia. Nik cares about you. I saw the way he kissed you before he left. I've never seen my brother act that way, ever. Matter of fact, I've never seen him with a woman for more than a night. He never brings them back to the house. You're special."

"I'm your best friend. He made it clear from the beginning that my place here was temporary. I never told you, but he planned to send me away as soon as I turned eighteen. Had I not taken that bullet for him, I would have been on a bus somewhere far away. Then whatever guilt he felt kept me here longer. Add in the sex and, well, he was always going to eventually become tired of me."

"Lia, that's not true. He doesn't—" She's cut off when the door opens again.

The brute of a man stands there, glaring at Ivanna, a fresh bandage on his arm.

"Don't move an inch. Boss wants you clean and ready for the stage." Leaning down, he swipes her mouth hard and fast, removing the blood from her lips.

He jumps back quickly, never taking his eyes off her. He looks at her as if she is a snake waiting to strike.

"You"—he points at me—"stand and come over here."

Swallowing hard, I use the wall to help me stand. I'm okay at first, but after two steps, I feel my legs start to give.

The man curses, stepping toward me to catch me.

"Useless fucking woman. Come on. We need to get you cleaned up and ready as well," he mutters, pulling me from the room. He closes the door, locking it with a key. I watch as he places them back in his right pocket.

He half drags me down the hall, passing several closed doors.

"What are those?" I ask, expecting him to tell me to shut up, but he doesn't.

He chuckles instead. "Those are the private rooms. I'm sure you'll find out what the inside of one looks like tonight. Very fun things happen there. I once saw a girl get strung up by her ankles while her master carved the alphabet into her skin. Fuck, it was hot the way she screamed," he says wistfully.

Chills cover my body as he uses one hand to adjust his very obvious hard-on.

What a sadistic bastard. Ivanna only wants to knock him out, but he deserves death. We can discuss that once we get there.

At the end of the hall, he turns left. I glance over my shoulder to look down the opposite hall.

"There's no escaping that way. You'll see that hall later when we escort you to the stage." He tugs me into a large room with showers along the far end of the wall. "Strip."

I want to fight back, but I force myself to relax. I can't fight back when I can barely stand.

"Can I have some water or something? I think I'm dehydrated."

"The showers have water. Now strip."

I bite my lower lip as I undress. I hate this. I hate the fact that this man is going to see an intimate part of me that I have sheltered my entire life. The only man I've ever let see me like this is Nikolai. Yet this man stands here, watching as I strip my clothes off. His eyes take in every single bare part of my body, cataloging it as if he plans to revisit it later.

My stomach rolls at the thought.

He grabs my arm, pulling me under one of the showerheads. I shriek when he turns it on, the cold water cascading over my body.

"There's soap in the dish. Wash your body and do so quickly."

I shiver as I grab the soap, doing as he asks. When I turn my back to him, I open my mouth, swallowing some of the water. It tastes metallic, but I need strength. If I'm truly dehydrated, drinking this will help get me some of my strength back.

I multitask by washing my body and drinking as much of the nasty water as I can. By the time I'm done with my body, I feel a little better.

Wetting my hair, I use the bar soap in it, knowing it will make my hair feel disgusting, but I do as he commanded anyway.

By the time the prison-like shower is complete, I'm much cleaner and a little stronger.

The man turns off the water, grabbing my arm to pull me toward a cabinet at the end.

"What size are you?"

"Depends on what it is," I tell him.

"Don't play dumb. You saw what she was wearing. What size?"

"My bra size is thirty-four B."

"Thank you for your cooperation." He digs through a couple before pulling out a red one. "This will look amazing against your skin."

He lays it on the bench before grabbing a towel.

"Hands out."

I do as he asks, my skin crawling as he takes his time drying every inch of my body. I don't miss the way his hand slips under the towel to touch my pussy or how he very obviously gropes at my breasts. I don't make a single move, though. I stare straight ahead at the wall, plotting the way I plan to murder him.

When he is finally done, he pulls the negligée over my head until it's in place.

"Maybe I'll place a bid on you myself. I doubt I'll win, but you are awfully sweet. You'll go for top dollar for sure. I bet Jakub will want a taste of you himself before you go on stage."

I swallow hard, trying not to react to his words. I remember how Jakub stared at me. He asked Nikolai for a taste, but he refused him. The only thing that saved me was my brand.

Reaching down, I brush the mark. I still hate what he did. Yeah, he asked for permission before, but he didn't give me all the facts. Then again, it's not like I asked and he didn't do it to hurt me. He was in a difficult situation and made a decision he thought was for the best. Somewhere along the way I've forgiven him but I won't forget. So much for being my protection. It doesn't even matter now.

"Let's get going. You'll be expected soon. The early auctions are almost done."

He leads me back out of the room, but a scream stops me in my tracks. I look ahead, seeing a very young girl being forced through the door of one of the rooms. She barely looks sixteen.

Fuck. We need to save her, too.

"Don't worry. She will be fine. I bet they will take very good care of her."

I let him continue to lead me, but I take note of which door she goes through. I can't save them all, but I will be taking her with me.

When we make it back to the room, he unlocks the door. As soon as it opens, movement catches my eye. Within seconds, the man is on the ground, Ivanna sitting on top of his chest with her hands around his neck.

"Help me," she says through gritted teeth.

I close the door, moving to grab one of his arms that is trying to knock her off him. He's struggling, but his head is bleeding. After several minutes, he finally goes slack.

"What did you hit him with?"

She laughs. "The piss bucket. Then I kneed him in the balls. Let's go."

I shake my head. "He needs to die. We can't leave him alive. It's too much of a risk. Plus, he's a sadistic asshole, and he touched me."

Ivanna's eyes widen. "Okay. How?"

"Search his pockets."

It takes several minutes, but I finally find a knife in his boot.

Thank you, Nikolai.

If I hadn't seen him pull one from there, I would have never thought to check his feet. Opening it, I hold it to the man's neck before hesitating.

Can I take this man's life?

"I can do it," Ivanna offers.

I shake my head. This man laughed about that young girl. He grew hard at the thought of another woman being mutilated.

I refuse to let him take another breath.

Quickly, I slice his neck, jumping back when blood spurts out.

"Are you okay?" Ivanna's voice is soft.

I turn to her. "I'm fine." Looking down at myself, I sigh.

All this blood will not go unnoticed.

"Maybe we can go back to the showers?" Ivanna murmurs as she takes in my body.

I shake my head. "No time. He said they would come for us soon. I want you to go. Get out of here and get Nikolai and Dimitri to come back for me. I saw them take a very young girl into a room down the hall. I'm going to go get her and then we will bunker down and wait for help to arrive."

"I can't leave you," Ivanna refuses.

"You can and you will. This is the only way."

She's shaky, but nods. "You better stay alive."

"Same goes for you."

Ivanna hands me the gun she took from the dead man at our feet. I grip it in one hand while holding the knife in the other.

Together, we quietly make our way down the hall. At the end, she goes right while I go left. I pause outside the door, pressing my ear to hear what is going on inside. I can only hear silence.

I watch as Ivanna gives me one last nod before stripping and stepping through the door.

The sound of chatter hits my ears before it blinks out with the closed door.

I wait a couple of minutes before I reach down for the door handle. I turn it slowly, letting out a breath when it doesn't seem to be locked.

Stepping into the room, I quickly close the door behind me as I take in the scene.

I was expecting several men as I watched at least three bring the girl in, but the room is empty except for a couple on the large bed in the middle.

The girl lies lifeless underneath the man thrusting inside of her.

I try to remain quiet as I move closer. I shove the gun between my breasts, deciding to use my knife instead. Nikolai never did get around to teaching me how to use one.

Ivanna taught me how to use a knife, though. Once I'm close enough, I strike, but the man catches a glimpse of me, jerking out of the way at the last second.

My knife skims his cheek, but now he stands naked in front of me.

"You want to play? Come on, let's play. I enjoy a little foreplay," the man's dark voice growls at me.

Then he lashes out, gripping my arm. Before I can stop it, my hand releases the knife, the sound of metal clattering on the ground. Then he spins me into his chest so that I'm facing away from him.

Pulling the gun from between my breasts, he tosses it toward the corner.

"I was getting pretty tired of the starfish on the bed. I prefer my women to have a little fight in them. Gets the blood flowing."

He rubs his erection against my ass, making me grit my teeth. I take two deep breaths, then I pull my head forward, jamming it back against his as hard as I can.

He curses out just as a sharp pain takes over my head. I fall to the floor, but I can't move right away. The ringing in my ears tells me I'm not at my best. I might not make it out of this.

I can feel the man jump on me as I try to clear the fuzziness in my head. After several moments, I can finally see straight. The man is running his hand over my body as his lips move with words I cannot hear.

I attempt to buck him off, but he is too heavy.

My heart pounds in my chest, making it ache as the realization dawns on me.

I have spent my entire life trying to avoid situations like this. I did everything I could to make a better life for myself. Yet still, I end up below a low life who thinks they can take what doesn't belong to him.

I'm about to head butt him again when a shot rings through the air, piercing through the ringing in my ear.

Then the man's face explodes.

CHAPTER NINETEEN

NIK

"We need to breach now. From what I can tell, most of the women have been sold already. Only a couple more until they get to the main attractions. Once that happens, we may not get to them in time," Alexei tells us from his perch across the street from Club Atlas.

"What's our best way in?"

He points toward the alley. "There is a door down there. I've seen several men knock on it to gain entry. I say I go down and see what the entrance fee is. Once I clear it, I'll wave you forward."

"Do you know where they are keeping them?"

Alexei pulls out a tablet, tapping on it a couple of times before he pulls out a blueprint.

"This is the main area. This is the stage they will show the product on. To the right, there is a door that leads to a couple of halls. My guess is they are in one of these rooms back here. From my research, I found that many of these are private rooms, but they also have empty rooms meant as cages. When we go through this door, we will have to cross the main room to get to them. You may be recognized, boss."

I consider his words. He's right. I will be recognized.

"Here's the plan. You two go through the back door. I'll wait three minutes before storming the front with the troops. Get them out of there quickly. Don't worry about us."

"Understood," they both say.

"Good. Now go."

I watch as Alexei goes down the alley. He knocks on the door and talks to the man for a minute. Then he punches the man before twisting his neck. He waves Dimitri forward before tossing the man in the alley.

I look at my watch and note the time.

After the longest three minutes of my life, I get on the radio to my men.

"We are storming the castle. No prisoners. Everyone in position?"

"Delta team one is a go."

"Alpha team one is a go."

"Bravo team one is a go."

"Charlie team one is a go."

"On the count of three. One. Two. Three."

I pull out my gun and take off running toward the front door as I see my team flank me. Shots ring out as the two guards at the door fall.

I fling the door open, firing two shots at the guards inside. As soon as they fall, more come running along with some of the patrons.

My men fill in beside me as we fire into the crowd. I wince when I see one of the women fall, but there is nothing I can do now. Pushing past them, I go farther into the club. My eyes land on the stage and I see red.

Ivanna is standing on the stage naked as a couple of men try to coax her into getting down. I aim my gun, shooting each man before looking back up at her.

Before I can say or do anything, Dimitri is up on the stage, flinging her over his shoulder as he takes off.

I let out the breath. One is safe. Now, where is Lia?

Movement in the VIP area catches my eye. Making the split decision to

NIKOLAI

leave Alexei to search the back rooms on his own, I head up to VIP.

Once at the top, I hear Oleg's voice loud and clear.

"You little punk. I brought you under my wing and you betray me for this Polish piece of shit. Where is she?"

"She is none of your concern. Now lower the gun before you end up dead, old man."

My stomach clenches at the voice.

Anton. He was the inside man the whole time. I vetted him. I trusted him.

Bursting into the room, I raise my gun. I spot several dead guards around the room. Oleg stands in the middle as Anton and Jakub share a couch, a shaking and naked woman between them.

"Well, what do we have here? A traitor, a Polish man, and a soon-to-be dead uncle. That sounds like the beginning of a bad joke."

"Nikolai, how nice of you to join us. I expected you sooner," Jakub says.

"Shut up. Tell me where she is. She's mine," Oleg sputters out.

The vein in his neck is pulsing as his blood pumps in anger.

Turning away from him, I address the traitor in the room. "What did he offer you? I mean, Felicity, I could see, but you kidnapped Ivanna. Did he offer you extra for her?"

Anton sneers. "He offered me a place in his ranks. I'm tired of the back and forth between you two. I need stable leadership."

I nod. "Understandable. Still unacceptable."

I shoot him in the leg, making him groan in pain.

"Do something," he says to Jakub.

He only shrugs. "You betrayed him. He's owed his pound of flesh. Now, if you are done, I'll tell you where your precious Felicity is. Ivanna may be lost, I'm afraid. She was on the floor when you burst in here."

"You kidnapped my niece? I will kill you." Oleg goes to step forward, but Jakub is faster. They grapple on the ground as I stand over them waiting them out. Might as well let them fight it out.

When the gun finally goes off, I point mine toward them.

Jakub stands, leaving Oleg gasping in pain on the floor. He turns to me, a smile on his face.

"Now, back to business. I will tell you where to find her in exchange, you open trade back up again. You honor the partnership we discussed when you were here before. You see, I knew you would come. This was the plan the whole time."

I consider him. "Alright. Take me to her."

He gestures for me to move forward, but I smirk at him. "No way. You first, buddy."

Anton yells behind us, "You're going to leave me here? What the fuck?"

"Good point." I turn toward the girl. "Run along, sweetheart. Go on."

As soon as she clears the room, I pick up my walkie-talkie. "Got a present for you in the VIP lounge."

Turning back, I smirk at Anton. "The men will take good care of you. You know how they love traitors."

As we walk away, I hear Anton screaming at us. I ignore him, pointing my gun into Jakub's back.

Most of the club is quiet now, my men having taken care of patrons and guards alike. Jakub leads me across the stage toward the door Alexei showed me. As we step through, we find silence.

"She should be in one of these rooms. You know I don't know why we haven't been partners this whole time. I knew that golden boy reputation was all for show. Your men weren't sure about your rule so you showed them kindness, leading different from your father. We both know that you are your father's son inside."

I scoff. "I'm nothing like that man. Now, which room is she in?"

Before he can speak, Alexei steps out of a room down the hall. He looks at me and gives me a curt nod.

He has her.

Knowing that, I turn to Jakub. Pressing the gun at the top of his spine, I smile.

"Seems our business has been concluded. See you in hell."

Pulling the trigger, I enjoy watching him jerk forward. I know I have paralyzed him from the neck down in one shot. If he survives, he won't have the same life he has led up to this point.

Looking back at Alexei, I growl at him, "Where is she?"

She steps out of the room, another woman on her arm. Ignoring the newbie, I stride toward my woman. Cupping her face, I press my lips to her, not even caring that she is covered in blood.

"*Kroshka.* My *kroshka*. Are you hurt? Do you need medical attention?" I ask, running my hands over her body, looking for where the blood has come from.

In my peripheral vision, I see Alexei take the woman from Lia and pull her to his chest. She stiffens, but lets him.

"I'm fine. This isn't my blood. I'm a little weak, but I'm okay," she reassures me. "What about Ivanna? Did you find her?"

I nod. "Dimitri has her."

"Boss, we should probably get out of here," Alexei says, breaking the moment.

I nod again. "Let's go."

A few steps forward, Lia sways. Not wanting to chance it, I pull her up into my arms, cradling her against my chest. Her arms wrap around my neck easily.

"I've got you, *kroshka*."

I meant it too. I would never let another person hurt my woman.

Never again.

Lia

I GO TO move off of Nik's lap as we pull into the estate.

"Stop trying to get away from me," he growls, and pulls me in closer.

"We're pulling up. It would be easier to get out if you aren't holding on to me," I point out.

"It will be fine," he says as the car comes to a stop.

I hear the driver's and passenger doors open and shut before our door is opened. Effortlessly, Nikolai slides out of the car while holding me.

"See." He smirks arrogantly, making me roll my eyes.

The front door flies open, and Ivanna comes barreling out of the house with Dimitri following behind.

"Lia! Are you okay?" she asks, voice filled with pain.

"I'm fine. This brute just refuses to put me down."

Ivanna ignores me, looking at Nikolai.

"None of the blood appears to be hers, but I want the doctor to check her over."

"Of course, we had him sent to her room," she says, falling into step with us.

Looking down at her, I notice she has already been tended to.

"What happened to your hand, Ivanna?" I ask.

She shrugs. "Broke my thumb to get out of the cuffs."

"Crazy bitch," I mumble, making Nikolai chuckle.

"What do you need me to do?" Dimitri asks as we walk inside.

"Check on the men. We need to know the status of those injured. I will visit the ones who perished families myself."

Dimitri breaks away at the base of the stairs.

"The doctor is unnecessary, really. I'm sure he's needed elsewhere," I murmur into Nikolai's chest.

"He's where he needs to be," he says at the landing of the stairs.

I see the doctor as soon as we walk into my room. Turning away from the window, he waves at the couch, telling Nikolai where he wants me. Wordlessly, Nikolai sits down in the chair with me in his lap.

"It might be easier if you take a step back, Nikolai."

"I won't let her go," he says, shaking his head.

I sigh and turn in his lap, facing the doctor. "Ignore him. Do what you need to do."

"Is any of the blood yours?" he asks as he puts on a pair of gloves. "Did you hit your head or anything?" he asks as he pokes and prods.

"I hit my head, but it doesn't hurt. I feel fine," I lie.

The doctor gives me a knowing look as he checks my eyes but doesn't say anything.

"I cannot do a full exam with you holding on to her like a barbarian, but from what I can tell, she will be fine. She will most likely have a couple bruises appear by morning and a headache," he says as he pulls his gloves off.

I feel Nikolai relax behind me, taking a deep breath.

"Thank you." His voice is quiet.

The doctor packs up his bag and nods as he leaves, shutting the door behind him.

"I need a shower."

Nikolai sighs, tapping the side of my leg. We both stand and he weaves his fingers through mine before pulling me toward the bathroom. Once inside, Nikolai turns on the water. Turning toward the mirror, I can't help but cringe.

I look like hell.

Nikolai comes up behind me, resting his hands on my hips, his eyes holding mine.

May I? he asks wordlessly.

I nod and Nikolai takes control, removing what little I have on. Through the mirror, I watch as his jaw twitches.

I turn in his arms, resting my hands on his chest. "I'm okay."

"You are. Now get in the shower and get cleaned up," he rasps.

I step into the shower and am instantly surrounded by warmth. I shut my eyes and tilt my head back, getting my hair wet.

"Will you join me?" My voice is small.

After a few moments of silence, Nikolai joins me in the shower, naked as the day he was born.

This isn't the way I imagined seeing him fully naked for the first time, but I'll take it.

Hell, it's not like anything about us is normal. We do everything in our own way.

Nikolai reaches for the shampoo, opening it and squirting some into his hand. After setting the bottle back down, he lathers the shampoo in his two big hands before massaging it into my hair. Keeping my eyes closed I wrap my arms around his waist, pressing us together, chest to chest. My breathing falls into sync with his as I rest my chin on his chest while he washes my hair.

"Tilt your head back."

I do as he says, loving the way it feels. When he reaches a particularly sore spot, I can't help but slightly tense, making him freeze.

I open my eyes.

"I'm fine. I promise," I reassure him.

Nikolai looks away as he reaches for the conditioner and starts the process all over again, before moving onto my body. I feel his cock hardening against my stomach as he washes me and it makes me want more. Makes me want him. Once he's done, he just holds me while tenderly running his hand along my lower back in a soothing motion.

I pull back slightly and stand up on my tiptoes, kissing the corner of his mouth, making him groan.

"This isn't the time, *kroshka*," he says, heat flashing through his eyes.

"Do you know what I thought about when I was locked in that room wearing barely anything?"

"What?"

"I thought about how I wanted you and only you. How I only wanted your hands touching me. Loving me. How we had wasted so much time being angry when we could have been together. When I could have given you everything. How good you could make me feel," I say, making him groan. "Will you, Nikolai? Will you touch me and make me yours? Will you make me feel good?"

Nikolai moves his hands lower, cupping below my ass before lifting me up and pressing me against a wall, making me gasp as I wrap my legs around his waist.

"If I touch you, *kroshka*, you will belong to me and only me. Can you handle that?"

"Yes…" I hiss as he rubs his cock along my slit.

"There will be no one else, ever. Do you understand?" he asks as he lays hot kisses along my neck.

"No one else, for either of us," I say as I rock my hips against him.

Nikolai removes one hand from my ass and shuts off the water, making me whimper.

"Don't worry, *kroshka*, I'll take care of you. We just need to move to where I can worship you all through the night. I will fuck you in the shower one day, but your first time should be special," he says as he steps out of the shower.

NIKOLAI

"How did you know?" I can feel my cheeks heating.

Nik walks straight to my bed, lying us both down.

"I've had my fingers and tongue inside you. Trust me, I knew."

I reach up kissing him. "I'm glad you'll be my first."

"And your last," he growls. "I wish we were in my room."

"Take me to your room then," I tell him.

He stands, wrapping the comforter around me before picking me back up.

It's only three steps from my room to his, but it feels like a million. I chuckle when I catch a glimpse of one of the guards doing a patrol. His eyes were wide before he turned around and headed the opposite way.

I'm sure Nikolai is a sight to see. He is buck naked, his dick pointing straight up.

Once in his room, his door slams behind us.

He lays me on the bed, removing the comforter like he's unwrapping a present.

"There's my beautiful *kroshka*."

When he smiles at me, I feel my heart grow warm. I meant what I said to him. I shouldn't have held out so long.

Truth is, I knew from the moment I saw him that I was going to lose myself to him one day. Even when he was going to force me away, something inside told me I was home.

"I'm going to make you feel so good, but I need to get you ready first, okay? It will hurt, but I want to make it hurt the least."

"I trust you," I tell him.

I realize in that moment that I mean it too. He might have made some mistakes, but I never wanted him to be perfect. All I wanted was for him to be mine.

My body shivers as he kisses his way down, pausing to nip at each of my nipples along the way. When he reaches my center, I cry out.

He doesn't take his time. He eats me like he is ravenous. As if he has been denied food for years.

My body arches into him, my hands burying themselves into his hair as I give in to the feelings he evokes in my body. With every swipe of his tongue, he erases all the horrors of the evening, replacing them with only the feeling of him.

The safe, warm feeling he leaves in me.

I know he should be out there being a boss to his men, but he's not. He's here with me. Making me feel good.

He is prioritizing me above the Bratva.

That thought along with his ministrations cause my body to convulse, giving in to the pleasure. I scream out his name so loud that my throat is raw when I finally stop.

He crawls up my body, his lips never leaving my skin.

"I love the way you sound when you come. It is music to my ears."

"I love you," I blurt out, then wince when I realize what I said.

He chuckles. "Open your eyes, Lia."

"I don't want to. Can we ignore that?" I ask, embarrassed.

His finger comes up to caress my cheek. "Open them."

Slowly, I peel my eyes open. Staring into his eyes, I see adoration reflected back at me.

"The way I feel about you, *kroshka*, cannot be expressed in words. Saying I love you is like saying the ocean is like a puddle. The comparison is nowhere near the truth. My feelings for you outweigh everything else in my life. You are more to me. Everything."

My heart hammers in my chest. I think he just admitted that he loves me.

No. He more than loves me.

"More," I murmur. "I like more."

"Me too. Now I'm going to make love to you so your first time is as special as you are to me, but tomorrow? Tomorrow I'm going to fuck you like I've wanted to do since the moment I saw you standing in my room that first time."

My core clenches at the thought. "Yes, sir."

He smiles. "I don't want to use protection with you. I'll pull out, okay?"

I nod. I should be starting my period in a couple days anyway, so we will be safe enough, but I make a mental note to ask the doctor for some birth control.

Nikolai presses his lips to mine, pressing his tongue into my mouth to caress mine. After a few moments, he presses forward, his cock against my center. He rubs back and forth for several minutes before pulling back. Then he reaches down to position himself at my entrance.

"Hold on to me. I'll go slow, but tell me to stop at any time. Got it?"

"Yes. Please. I need you," I tell him.

NIKOLAI

He smiles at me before pressing in slowly.

Fuck. I didn't realize it would burn so bad. He continues to slowly press in, his eyes locked on mine. When he is about halfway, he pulls back out before moving back in. He gives me a couple of short, slow thrusts before he thrusts hard once.

I feel a pinch of pain, but as he stills, I can't help the happiness I feel inside. Tears prickle my eyes, making his soften.

"Are you okay?" He leans down, kissing each eye before pressing kisses all over my face.

"I'm fine. Emotional I think. I'm happy it's you, Nikolai."

He pulls back, showing me the unfiltered emotions on his face. His own happiness is a mirror of my own.

My core clenches against him, making his cock jerk in response.

"Fuck, Lia. That felt good. Do it again."

So I do, making him groan.

"Move, Nikolai. Make love to me."

And he does. It's slow and sensual as his lips mark my body anywhere they can reach. He is in no hurry. He continues to press into me until the burn has faded, leaving only pleasure as our bodies connect in a way that I never could have imagined.

When his pace starts to pick up, he whispers in my ear, "I'm not going to last much longer, *kroshka*. You feel too good and I've wanted this for much too long. I need you to come for me."

Reaching between us, his finger starts to press against my clit until my body reaches its high. As I clench around him, he curses before pulling out to jerk himself over me. When he comes, it splashes all over my stomach.

"I love you, *kroshka*. Always and forever."

I smile in response, words escaping me.

After he cleans me up and tucks me into his side, I whisper his sentiment back to him as I fall asleep.

"Always and forever."

CHAPTER TWENTY

Lia

When I awake in the morning, the first thing I notice is the way my whole body aches. Some of it is from the fight the night before, but when I clench my core, I know that most of that is from what I shared with Nikolai.

Sitting up, I look around for him, but I don't find him. Instead, I find a bottle of pain reliever, a glass of water, and a note.

Needed to take care of business. Be back soon. Take two of these.
Love Nik.

My heart swells. I imagine him considering how to sign it. I don't think Nikolai has ever signed anything with "love."

Taking the pills, I pull myself out of bed. When I make it into the bathroom, I look at myself in the mirror.

I know nothing has really changed, but looking at my reflection, I feel like I have. I feel different.

I take in my body, ignoring the bruises, but focusing on the red marks that

Nikolai left along my body. My core clenches at the thought of his lips and teeth on my skin. I run my hands along my skin, marveling at the way my body feels when I think about him. I run my fingers through my sex, hissing at the mixture of pleasure and pain.

I'm sore, but I also feel excited.

I want him again. Right now.

"*Kroshka?*" I hear his voice as if I summoned him.

"In here," I call out to him.

He opens the bathroom door, his eyes heating as soon as he takes my naked body in. When his eyes reach my hand between my legs, he tsks me.

"Are you starting without me?"

His tone is teasing, but I'm not in a teasing mood.

"I need you, Nikolai."

His eyes darken, all humor fading into hunger.

"Are you sore?"

"Yes, but I ache for you. I need you."

"What do you need? Tell me."

"I need to feel you inside me. Now, Nikolai."

He moves to me, his fingers trailing down my arm until they meet my own at my pussy. He circles them around before pressing his two inside alongside my two. I gasp at the slight burn, but also the pleasure of being full again.

I never realized how amazing it would feel to have something inside.

No, not something. Him. I need him inside.

"Fuck, you are so wet." He kisses me hard before pulling back.

"Come back." I pout.

"Hush. I have a bunch of men waiting for me downstairs, so we need to make this quick."

I watch as he strips before making his way back over to me. "Hands on the counter. Bend over and show me that ass."

My body trembles at his words, but it obeys. I place my hands on the counter, sticking my ass up at him. Then I meet his eyes in the mirror.

Fuck, this is erotic as fuck. I can't even help myself. I moan at the sight.

"You are the most gorgeous woman I have ever laid my eyes on. Seeing you spread out for me, needing me inside to make you feel better. It does something to a man. You fucking own me, *kroshka*."

His words are like a balm to my soul. I'm glad I own him because he has owned me for a long while, even if I hated to admit it.

His hand caresses down my spine, coming to rest against my ass. With one quick strike, his palm lands on my ass, making me moan.

"My baby likes to be spanked. Isn't that right?"

"Nikolai, I thought we were in a rush. I want you. Get inside me or I'll finish myself."

He smacks me again. "I'm in control here, Lia. Let me savor the moment."

Pressing my forehead into the counter, I take a deep breath. I don't know how much more anticipation I can take.

Before I resort to begging, his hand curls into my hair, pulling my head up as his other positions himself at my entrance.

"Watch us. Watch what you do to me."

Then he slams inside me. I cry out at the sudden invasion, but my center is clenching, so close to release already.

"Fuck, you fit me like you were made for me. You were sent here just for me. Isn't that right, *kroshka*?"

I hum my approval, losing all ability to form a coherent sentence as he starts to piston his hips, his dick gliding in and out, hitting me deeper than last night.

This is the fuck he promised me. It's hot, dirty, and quick.

When his hand readjusts from my hair to my neck, I about come from the new sensation. I knew I liked his hand on my throat from before, but when he applies a little pressure as his cock strokes every inch of my pussy, I'm unable to hold back. I scream out as my body milks him for everything he has.

He barely pulls out in time, spilling his release all over the small of my back and ass. I feel the warm liquid trickling down between my ass cheeks.

Nikolai is breathing heavily as he drags his fingers in the cum, bringing it to my mouth. I open obediently, licking his fingers clean.

"Fuck, that's how. I'm going to fuck every single hole in your body one day. I'm going to know what every single inch of you feels like."

"Please," I moan out my approval.

He chuckles before slapping my ass, making me yelp.

"Get cleaned up, then go eat. Ivanna is waiting for you. I'll come see you when I'm done with my men."

He pulls me up then, turning me to press a soft kiss against my lips.

Then he grabs his clothes, retreating to the bedroom.

I sigh in contentment as I turn the shower on.

I love that man.

NIK

I WASN'T PLANNING on fucking Lia, but fuck if she didn't look hot as fuck standing in the mirror touching herself.

Then she begged me to fuck her and I couldn't help myself.

If she begged me like that, she could get me to do just about anything for her. Fuck, she has me by the balls.

Dimitri said it from the beginning. He could see it before I could.

Pulling my clothes on, I quickly make my way out of the bedroom. I heard the shower turn on, tempting me to join her, but I can't.

I've made my men wait long enough.

Making my way downstairs, I stop off in the dining room.

Maxim and Ivanna are seated at the table chatting while waiting on Lia.

"She will be down in a moment. I'll be back later."

"Is she okay?" Ivanna asks, worry in her eyes.

"She's more than okay. I promise." I wink, making her cringe.

"Disgusting. Go away please."

I only laugh louder at that, tapping my knuckles on the doorframe twice before leaving.

It's amazing what some good sex with a woman you love can do for you. I feel like I'm on cloud nine as I exit the house to find Dimitri and a large group of my men waiting for me.

"Thank you all for being here. We appreciate all the work you have been doing. However, there was a breach of trust within the ranks. While we know that because there is one bad apple, the rest of the bunch may be fine. We do not want any other infected to remain in our ranks. With that being said, the men who were at the club last night decided they wanted the punishment for the defector to be a group activity and have brought him to the warehouse. Who would like to show the traitor what happens when those we trust betray us?"

When every single hand raises, I nod.

"Good. I never wanted to breed loyalty from fear. There should be a mutual trust between us in order for this to work. I am going to be implementing some new policies and tests to show loyalty. It will be tedious, but it will also help keep us all safe. I care about each and every one of you as individuals. You are not just a number to me. I don't want to bury you. We will mourn those we lost last night and have a ceremony for them later this week. For now, head over to the warehouse."

After they disperse, Dimitri comes to my side.

"Are you going to go with them?"

"I should, but I also want to be here for Lia. You should go."

He shakes his head. "No, you need to go. Go be with our men. I'll stay with the girls. They will be safe."

The possessive part of me doesn't want to leave her, but I know he is right.

"Okay. I want updates the entire time I'm gone."

"Understood."

Leaving her goes against my natural instincts, but I do it.

When I reach the warehouse, I know I made the right decision. My men are waiting for me.

Walking inside, I pat each one I pass on the shoulder.

Once inside, I look to the traitor in question. He is already roughed up, but alive.

When he looks up at me, he winces.

"Your fate has been decided by your peers. I'm not here to participate. I'm here to witness." Turning to the man standing guard, Yury. "Have you decided his fate?"

"Yes, sir. He will suffer from a cut from each man in attendance."

I nod. "Very well. Get on with it."

I stand back, proud as I watch each man step forward, knife in hand to cut Anton. I ignore his cries of pain or the ashen look on his face as blood pours from his skin.

Some go deeper than others, but they are all respectful enough to make sure he will live.

When the final one is done, I turn to the group.

"Traitors are not only a disgrace to me, but to our organization. If you cannot trust the brother next to you to have your back, then what is the point of even being here. Anton turned on you. You have seen what happens when that happens. Yury, make sure the trash is taken care of."

As I walk out, I hear the group of men lose all sense of humanity, tearing the traitor limb from limb as they all get their pound of flesh.

I should get mine as well, but all I can think about is her.

Kroshka.

EPILOGUE

SIX MONTHS LATER

NIK

"Ivan's requesting additional resources in Chicago. Seems the Yakuza have been making things a little difficult for him lately."

Dimitri sits next to me in the back seat of the town car as we head toward tonight's meeting. It's been six months since everything with the Polish went down, but they have finally determined a new leader.

The only problem is that it is Jakub's brother, Jan.

I scoff. "That sounds like a personal problem. He shouldn't have pissed off the dark prince if he didn't want things to be difficult for him. Deny his request. I'm not getting involved."

"Got it. One last thing" —Dimitri clears his throat— "I have assigned a couple of my men to watch the girls when they start classes next month."

I chuckle, shaking my head. I've been letting Dimitri take on more responsibility. Allowing him to cultivate his own group of men separate from mine. Sure, they all still answer to me, but after the Ivan situation in Chicago with the Yakuza, I realized I needed more eyes on the men. I just don't have the time to spend with them like I used to.

I have also had Maxim doing the same thing. As my third in command, I want him to have his own men as well. It killed me to pull him off of Lia, but she understood. She doesn't want to hold him back.

As for me, I'm cultivating a new group of men under me. I don't fully trust them yet, but I allowed Lia to choose her own personal guard. He seems to be doing well enough.

"You mean you won't be sitting through boring lectures to keep her on a tight leash?"

He huffs. "Not likely. Unless this meeting turns out differently than we think. She drives me insane."

I smirk at him. "You wouldn't have a thing for my sister, would you?"

It's not the first time I've thought it. Most men would probably kill him for the suspicion alone, but Ivanna was never going to marry a good boy. No, she will marry a Bratva man. Even if it's not arranged, she wouldn't be able to cope in a normal life.

If I had to choose for her, Dimitri would be the only one I trust with her.

"Not in a million years. She's a damn menace. You know she texted me telling me she's staying at a hotel tonight and demanded I escort her there. Who the fuck does she think she is?"

"Princess Ivanna, of course. Did she say why she wants to go to a hotel? Maybe she's planning to make a move on you."

"God, I hope not. You know, when she was fifteen, she made a pass at me. When I turned her down, she became this unbearable tantrum-throwing girl."

I shake my head. "You broke her young heart. What did you expect?"

"For her to realize that she was a child and there was no way I could think of her as anything other than a job."

I snort. "She's eighteen now. What's stopping you?"

"Just because you got yourself a barely legal vixen doesn't mean I need one. Besides, that ship has sailed. I think she would rather stab me at this point. Fuck, women are complicated."

NIKOLAI

I shrug. "She will pick someone someday."

He growls, "I'll kill him before he gets the chance."

I chuckle lightly, but grow somber as we approach the building.

Club Atlas has been shut down since we took the Polish out, yet Jan still wanted to meet here.

It stirs up a rage in my gut at the thoughts of what we found here. Ivanna naked, running for her life while Lia was in the back, saving another young woman's life, equally as exposed.

I'll never forget the feeling of fear of losing her I felt that day. Nor the immense relief as soon as she was back in my arms.

It was then I knew I could never let her go.

"Maxim, everything set?" I ask the man in the driver's seat.

"Yes, boss."

His men are fanned out in the neighboring buildings, ready to intervene if needed. Dimitri's men are with the girls.

"Let's get this over with then," I tell them both.

Maxim gets out to come open my door. I slide out as Dimitri comes to my side from behind the car.

I stare up at the building for a moment.

Then I head inside, my men flanked on either side of me.

At the door, two men stand, nodding to me as they open the club doors.

For a moment, I almost expect to hear the loud music and chatter from before. Not tonight, though. The club is empty, many of the chairs still overturned from the fight that occurred. Hell, there is glass littering the floor still.

Walking through the club, I make my way up to the VIP level. Once there, I'm disgusted to see the blood still staining the velvet couches lining the wall.

Jan stands beside a table with two chairs that were obviously arranged for this meeting. Sitting on the table is a bottle of top-shelf vodka and two glasses.

"Nikolai, what a pleasure to finally meet you. I apologize it has taken so long to arrange this meeting. I had some cleaning to do, as you can see." He gestures to the club.

I nod. "I appreciate you reaching out. My condolences on the loss of your brother."

He chuckles. "He was an idiot. Good riddance, if you ask me."

Maybe we will get out of this without bloodshed tonight.

I nod my head in response, not having anything nice to say about the man. Jan might be portraying that he does not care about his brother's death, but only a fool would speak ill of the dead in front of their family members.

"Have a seat. Let's have a drink. We have much to discuss."

I take a seat, knowing my men will stand by the entrance, taking in the surrounding area.

"What are your plans?" I ask him as he pours us each a drink.

As he finishes, he hands me a glass before taking a sip of his own. He is quiet for several moments before finally speaking.

"I don't plan to continue this venture my brother sought here in the city and through your territory. He was greedy."

"He pushed for more than I was willing to give and conspired behind my back to take it by force."

"I think it's best if we keep our current territories separate. That's why I asked you here" —he gestures to the club— "I do not plan to reopen this establishment. I feel it would be in poor taste."

I narrow my eyes in suspicion. "What will you do instead?"

"Rebuild on the other side of town and filter our product through the cartel's territory. I have already struck up a bargain with them. We will still use this part of the territory, but not for this particular branch of our business."

I think it over. "What do you want?"

"I want the war to end. We have lost many men on our side. I know that you have still been pursuing any men involved with this place. You have taken most of them out already, but I ask that you stop your hunt. The men who were assigned here were only doing the job they were ordered to do. I believe enough bloodshed has occurred to sate your need for vengeance."

I grit my teeth. "Do not tell me what will sate my vengeance. Your brother kidnapped my sister and woman and attempted to sell them."

"I'm aware. That is why I offer you this compromise. We move our less enjoyable part of our business away from your land and, as a show of good faith, we will burn this building down. In exchange, all I ask is that you pull your dogs off my men. Let me build a new relationship with you. One where we maintain our business separately, but peacefully."

I think it over for a moment. "Alright. I can agree to that."

"Great. I have one more present for you. He will be delivered to your car upon your departure. I hope it shows that I mean what I say."

He leans forward to shake my hand. I shake his as well before standing.

"Thank you for the invitation and compromise," I tell him, setting my untouched drink back on the table.

He eyes it a moment before nodding. "Thank you for accepting. Please do not hesitate to reach out if you need anything in the future. Treat this as a fresh slate."

"You as well," I tell him before turning to leave.

When we reach the car, my eyes widen.

Charles, Lia's foster father who attempted to rape her, stands at the back of our car held between two guards, tied up and looking worse for the wear.

Why would he deliver this man up on a silver platter?

Not willing to allow this opportunity to pass me up, I nod as Maxim pops the trunk.

I wait until we are settled into the car before I speak.

"I don't trust that man one bit. Make sure Alexei keeps eyes on him."

Lia

STANDING ON THE balcony, I smile at the sky. The stars are beautiful tonight. Even being in the middle of a pretty residential area, Nikolai has created a utopia inside the walls of the compound for us.

It seemed almost like a prison before, but now he has added more flowers to the land. Not only that, but he only has lights on the wall now, allowing for some of the light pollution to dissipate so that I could see the stars again.

My phone dings, making me smile.

They are here.

Ivanna is at the front door with her bag packed. She has been amazing. When I asked her to get Dimitri out of the house tonight, she didn't hesitate. Then she helped me set this whole thing up.

Nikolai asked me to move into his bedroom full-time six months ago, but I wasn't ready. How could I be? My whole life, anything I have truly loved has been taken from me.

I mean, he tells me he loves me, but that small, insecure part of me always questioned it.

That was, until this morning.

I don't know if it was his first time doing it or only the first time I've caught him, but he surprised me.

I heard his alarm go off, but instead of falling back into a deep sleep like I normally do, I'd lay in bed, half awake as I listened to the shower run. I didn't move when he came out, moving about the room quietly to get ready for his day.

Then, right before he left, he came and sat on the edge of the bed. He brushed a piece of hair from my face before leaning down to press a kiss to my forehead, then my lips.

Then he whispered in my ear.

"I love you, kroshka and I cannot wait to get back to you. I'll miss you all day."

Then he kissed me one last time before leaving the room.

He didn't say those pretty words for me to hear per se. He said them because he meant them. I knew in that moment that I needed to squash my insecurities and give him everything.

So I did. After I was sure he was gone, I went about moving my things into his room. Half of his closet and dresser were already cleared out, as if he was only waiting for me to take the final step.

When Ivanna found out what I was doing, she was ecstatic and happily helped me finish up.

I can hear the door to the room open, making me smile. He will be wondering where I am.

"Kroshka?" he calls out.

I smile to myself, slipping in through the balcony door.

He stiffens a moment before his eyes take me in.

"Why are the lights off?" he asks.

I flip the light on his desk on. He smiles when he takes me in.

I dressed for the occasion. A tight white tank top and sleep shorts, just like the night we met.

"What are you doing?" He steps toward me.

"The night I slipped into your room, I thought I was dead for sure. Honestly, I was okay with it, though. I had been fighting for so long to survive that I had given up. If God was going to take me, I wanted it to be you that ended it. At least it wasn't that bastard. Then I woke up, and my entire life had changed. I don't know why you chose me, but you gave me a new reason to live. You offered me a whole new life and because of that, I will be forever grateful. I've moved all of my things in here. I want forever. With you. If you still want it."

He keeps moving toward me until he stands in front of me. Gently, he brushes the back of his hand across my cheek. When he speaks, he doesn't say what I think he will. "We got him. Tonight."

My eyes widen. "What?"

"Charles. We got him. He's gone."

I frown. "Death seems too easy for him."

He chuckles, leaning in to kiss me. "I never said he was dead, *kroshka*. Only that he is gone. He will never hurt you or anyone else again. I will always protect you. You know that, right?"

"I do."

"Good, because while I changed you, you also changed me. I love you. Forever."

"I love you."

I cannot wait to spend my forever with this man.

You know, my mom was right. He is no prince charming, but he is a wicked prince that was made just for me.

ONE YEAR LATER

Lia

"What are you and Nik doing tonight?" Ivanna asks as we put our things in our bags at the end of class.

"As far as I know, we're staying in tonight. Unless something has changed since this morning." I put my bag over my shoulder.

"Ivanna," someone calls out, making us turn.

An attractive guy with brown hair approaches us with a smile on his face as he looks at my best friend.

"Hey Kyle," she says with a small smile on her face as she tucks her hair behind her ear.

"I was wondering, would you like to go out sometime?" he asks bashfully.

Ivanna ducks her head, peeking at me out of the corner of her eye. "Yeah, I think I would."

"Tonight too soon?"

"I'm free tonight. What time are you thinking?"

He adjusts the strap of his bag as he tries to not smile. "Would seven or eight work for you? Maybe we could have dinner?"

"That works for me."

"Sweet, can I get your number?"

"Ivanna," I say, getting her attention, nodding toward the door. Dimitri is standing there waiting for us.

She rattles off her number as she reaches for my hand, pulling me away.

"What was that about?" Dimitri asks as we approach.

"Nothing," Ivanna says, pulling me past him.

Once we exit the building, she weaves her arm through mine and looks over her shoulder to make sure Dimitri and Andrei, my guard who replaced Maxim, aren't too close.

"I can't believe he asked me out," she says softly.

"Guy has had eyes for you all semester," I point out.

"True. You know I had that group project with him a while back and he was so sweet."

"Dimitri won't like it."

"Yeah, well Dimitri can fuck off." She sighs. "Will you help me sneak out?"

I pause. "I don't know how I feel about you going off with someone completely alone, Ivanna."

"Come on," she begs. "It will be fine. I promise. If it makes you feel better, I will send you a picture of his license plate and driver's license before I get in the car. I'll make sure my tracking app is on for you, so if anything happens, you will know where I am."

I sigh as I think about it.

"I just really want a night to myself where I can be a normal college girl. Dimitri scares every guy off and I really like Kyle."

"If he's worth it, he will have to get used to Dimitri and the men in our life." I bite my lip. "But just this once, I will help you," I say, making her squeal. "Seriously though, I need you to send me the pictures and keep me updated. We both know they will notice you're gone sooner rather than later and I need to make sure my ass is covered."

"Thank you, thank you!" she says, hugging me as we walk. "Now, what should I wear?"

NIK

"Hey," Lia says softly, making me look up.

I watch her shut the door and can't help but smirk.

"Is it time?" I ask, tossing my pen onto my desk as she walks toward me.

As she walks around my desk, I push back from the desk. Lia puts her hands on my shoulders, straddling my lap, sitting.

"How was your day?" I ask as my hands find her hips.

"Good." She smiles. "Any issues today?"

"Everything went smoothly," I say, referring to Bratva business.

I weave my hand into her hair, pulling her lips down to mine, kissing her. Lia rocks her hips against me, making me grow hard.

"Can I help you, *kroshka*?" I murmur against her lips.

"I don't know, you tell me," she teases, rocking into me again.

I stand, making her wrap her legs around my waist and walk over to the couch in my study. I lay Lia down, hovering above her. My hand goes to the zipper of her shorts as I kiss down her neck. Lia unbuttons her top as I slide her shorts off. Leaning down, I take her nipple into my mouth, making her whimper as she arches into me, weaving her hand into my hair.

"Do you need me?" I ask as I stroke her lips.

"You know I do."

The door to the study ricochets off the wall, making me drop down onto Lia, covering her.

"Where is she?" Dimitri demands, looking frazzled.

"Dimitri," I growl.

Once he gets a good look at us, he groans, turning his back to us. Giving us some sort of privacy.

"I know you know where she is, Lia," he says as he runs his hands through his hair.

"Get out, Dimitri. Or else I'll have to kill you."

He growls, "Not until she tells me where to find Ivanna."

I pull back slightly, raising a brow, silently asking Lia what's going on.

"She's safe. I promise," she says as she strokes my back.

"No, she's not. Ivanna isn't here and I'm not with her," he hisses.

"Show some respect, Dimitri," I warn before turning back to the woman under me. "Explain."

"A guy we go to school with asked her on a date and she accepted."

"And why would she go without telling me or taking Dimitri or one of his men?"

"Because she wanted one night to be a normal nineteen-year-old girl, Nikolai." Lia sighs. "Dimitri would sit there and scare the guy away like he has with the others. Before she left, I made her send me a picture of his driver's license and license plate. Her tracker is on, and she's supposed to text me often."

"Lia, you know we have these rules for a reason," I chastise.

"I know you do, but you also need to trust Ivanna. She's nobody's victim. Let her prove it to you," she pleads, giving me those big hazel eyes.

"What time is she supposed to be back?" I ask.

"Dinner is at eight. Give her until midnight."

"Midnight?" Dimitri says, sounding outraged.

"Dimitri, pull up her tracker. You can sit outside the restaurant and watch, but do not let yourself be seen. Then follow her home." As soon as the order is out of my mouth, he's out of the room, shutting the door behind him.

"Tell me, *kroshka*, how did she get out unnoticed?"

"The same way I broke in." She smiles wickedly.

"You know I have to punish you for this, right?"

"Oh?" she says, faking outrage.

"I'm going to drag it out all night long," I say as I slip a finger inside of her, making her hiss.

"Totally worth helping her sneak out," Lia pants next to me, making me laugh.

If this year is anything to go by, life with Lia will never be boring.

The End.

THANK YOU!

Thank you for reading Nikolai. We hope you loved this story as much as we do. Want more Syndicates Series? Check out, Enzo available now on Amazon and Kindle Unlimited.

Want to stay up to date on our newest releases and access to exclusive content? Sign up for our newsletter now!

AUTHOR BIO

Cala Riley, better known as Cala and Riley, are a pair of friends with a deep-seated love of books and writing. Both Cala and Riley are happily married and each have children, Cala with the four-legged kind while Riley has a mixture of both two-legged and four. While they live apart, that does not affect their connection. They are the true definition of family. What started as an idea that quickly turned into a full-length book and a bond that will never end.

Acknowledgements

Husbands/Family- Thank you for loving us through the crazy and listening to us ramble.

Ashley Estep- Thank you for staying on us to make sure we stayed on schedule.

Louise O'Reilly- Thank you for being you.

Jenny Dicks- Thank you for all the swoons & ideas.

Aimee Henry- Thank you for joining the team.

Nikki Pennington- For listening to our rambles and talking us off of ledges.

My Brothers Editor/ Elle- Thank you for being the most laid back editor and making the entire process painless.

Books n Moods- Thank you for everything that you do for us. From covers to formatting and just being a cheerleader in our corner.

Bloggers/Readers- Thank you for loving our stories as much as we do and spreading the word.

Also by Author

Brighton Academy Series
Unbidden
Unpredictable
Undeniably
Unapologetically

Mafia Royalty Series
Mafia King
Mafia Underboss
Mafia Prince

The Syndicates
Matteo
Killian
Haruaki
Nikolai
Enzo

Trailer Park Girls Duet
Mayhem
Harmony

Shadow Crew Series
Redlined
Friction
Shift
Finish Line

Standalone
One of Them Girls

Where to Find Us

Facebook
Instagram
Tiktok
Bookbub
Goodreads
Amazon
Cala Riley's Boudoir of Sin
Website
Newsletter

Printed in Dunstable, United Kingdom